I0748497

First Edition published November 17, 2021
by Indies United Publishing House, LLC

ISBN: 978-1-64456-396-0 [Hardcover]
ISBN: 978-1-64456-397-7 [Paperback]
ISBN: 978-1-64456-398-4 [Mobi]
ISBN: 978-1-64456-399-1 [ePub]

*Contrary to popular belief at the Library of Congress, this is not, in fact, a comic book or graphic serialized novel, but we hope you will enjoy it anyway.

INDIES UNITED PUBLISHING HOUSE, LLC
P.O. BOX 3071
QUINCY, IL 62305-3071
www.indiesunited.net

Dedicated to every person who ever took a chance on an unknown author.

Thank you.

Table of Contents

INDIES UNITED PUBISHING HOUSE
PRESENTS

A MULTI-AUTHOR ANTHOLOGY

INDIES UNITED PUBLISHING HOUSE, LLC

Foreword

Jayne Southern

'Stories are neither fact nor fiction. They're greater than that – they are allegories, philosophical treatises and fables that hold the potentional to entertain, reveal and instruct.' – Imani Perry, Hughes-Rogers Professor of African American Studies at Princeton University and author.

Storytelling can be traced back to ancient legends, mythology, folklore, and fables found in communities all over the world. Stories existed before humans could write; Irish, African, Jewish, American Indian and many other cultures are testimony to the importance of these oral traditions. These stories were passed down, generation by generation, verbatim in most cases, to secure the history of the people; they also enhanced developmental skills, memory, bonding , communications skills – and imagination.

The advent of writing added another dimension: the preservation of cultural and tribal history, legends, mythic tales, folk stories, fairy tales and family stories. Imagination combined with writing opened a new dimension for reminisces and new stories. Printing opened vast dimensions for sharing stories and legends.

Short stories as we know them today emerged in the early 19th century. Margaret Attwood, James Baldwin, Ernest Hemingway, Alice Munro, Tobias Wolff, Shirley Jackson,

Jhumpa Lahiri , Mary Shelley, Katherine Mansfield, Neil Gaiman, Louisa May Alcott are just a few of those who have perfected the short story.

What is the importance of stories? Every story helps us explain experience, to make cognitive and emotional links that help shape how we view the world and life. Think of the importance of fairy tales to children, how they prepare them for what they will encounter as they grow. Stories cover everything from wicked stepmothers to science, memories, humour, horror, science fiction, thrills, spills and salvation. It's worth taking the time to read *The Uses of Enchantment* by Bruno Bettelheim.

Writers of short stories draw from all genres, all literary techniques. The vital ingredients of character, setting, conflict, plot and theme are united with pitch, pace, passion (not necessarily rumpy-dumpy!), poetry and precision, much in the way poetry is constructed. Only certain words will work, in a certain order. Short stories are not 'dashed off'.

Writers hone their skills with short stories to offer a brief engagement with an event, a character, a mood, a memory, an imagining, as emotive and affecting as any novel. Short stories offer readers the opportunity to explore new writers, to tempt readers to invest in their novels. The frisson of a good story can entertain, inform, alarm, cheer, move to empathy or tears, or simply provide a pleasurable twenty-minute read. Gifts not to dismiss.

Indies United Publishing House has an enviable camaraderie of writers in a splendid range of genres. The stories in this edition are but a tasty morsel to enjoy!

You can consider escaping to the moon, or remember the exquisite pain of first love and celebrating our differences. Restoring your faith in your fellow man by reading of the extraordinary kindess of strangers will remind you of unexpected generosity you have experienced. Maybe the mind numbing take on transformation and power of the mind – sometimes negative – will give you pause for thought. Reflections on childhood time with parents and grandparents will bring back memories too good not to savour and carry with you.

I have been fortunate to work with many authors, in a broad spectrum of fiction and non-fiction and never fail to wonder at how they work such magic with the same twenty-six letters and a handful of punctuation marks. The depth and breadth of a writer's work, the originality, the research, the commitment to putting their imaginings to paper, the courage in placing manuscripts with agents, editors, proofreaders, publishers, reviewers and you, the reader, is nothing short of astonishing.

Enjoy the latest anthology from Indies United Publishing House.

'The writer does not and should not have the last word. That belongs to the reader.' – Tobias Wolf

A Froggy Distraction

By Timothy R. Baldwin

My earliest memories of catching frogs are set in the foreground of my grandparent's camp, their marshy lawn sloshing on my shoes and soaking my socks.

One afternoon my grandmother took me outside to play a game of scoop ball. This game is played using scoop bats, which resemble a lacrosse stick, only small enough to be held and used with one hand. As my grandmother and I tossed the ball with our scoop bats, my brother remained inside. There, I imagine he sat in the dim light of the kitchen, refusing to eat the soup my grandparents made for lunch that day. Clearly not my parent's cooking, the homemade soup consisted of a watery broth, various vegetables, and tiny shreds of chicken. I had initially complained about the food.

"It's too watery," I had said as I stirred pieces of mushy carrots and soggy celery around the tasteless broth. "I thought it would be thicker, like stew."

"Well, it's not," my grandfather barked. "Eat it."

My brother curled his lips and glared. "No."

"Well, I guess you two will just sit there until you eat it," my grandmother said.

Presented with no other option, I managed to down the food without further complaint. My brother was not as cooperative. On top of being a picky eater, he possessed an iron-clad will that needed to be coaxed, rather than forced open. My grandfather, never the coaxing type, remained inside waging a war of wills with my brother.

Meanwhile, my grandmother and I went outside. She'd toss a whiffle ball toward me. I'd extend my scoop bat and once again fail to catch the ball. Though countless times my grandmother would tell me to get in front of the ball, my feet would remain firmly planted in the marshy ground. Then I'd overthrow the ball, paying for my carelessness by running after it and trying it again.

Eventually, the screen door opened with a creak to reveal my brother, lips drawn tight as he promenaded down the steps. Behind him, the door swung shut. A giant hand caught the door and my grandfather, pushing the door open, tramped down the steps after my brother.

"Hey, Peter," my grandfather barked. "You didn't finish."

"Let him alone for now," my grandmother said as my brother put distance between himself and my grandfather.

"Eh? Well, he won't get anything later."

"Why don't you wait inside on the porch."

Tromping back inside, my grandfather plopped himself on a dingy-white wicker chair as he waited for my grandmother. Meanwhile, my grandmother showed my brother how to use the scoop ball. For a moment, she watched us toss and miss the ball several times before one landed with a satisfying thwack into my scoop. Apparently satisfied, my grandmother joined my grandfather on the porch. As my brother and I silently tossed and overthrew the ball, we could hear the muffled whispers of my grandmother and my grandfather's voice, which seemed unable to achieve a volume lower than a suppressed roar.

Deciding we had enough of the game, my brother and I set the ball and scoop bats down in favor of an exploration of the yard. A clothesline seemed to curtain the yard in, especially with a white sheet draped over the line and flapping in the breeze. Beyond the white curtain, there was a brown boat shed.

From there, a dock led toward the lake. As we walked toward the boat shed, my brother and I discovered the drainage ditch, a barrier between my grandparents' yard and their neighbor's yard. Walking toward the drainage ditch, droplets of water splashed up from the ground, dampening my socks and legs. As I took another step, hundreds of frogs leaped into the air and away from my deadly feet. Stopping, I placed my hands on my knees to examine my find. I called my brother over.

"Peter, come here."

Trotting and splashing, my brother created living waves in the marshy drainage ditch as frog after frog leapt toward me.

"I want to catch one," my brother said as both of his hands snatched at the water in front of him, causing a frog to leap a safe distance away from him. Splashing another heavy foot down in front of him, he executed the same motion which resulted in the same outcome, hands filled with grass and mud, but no frog. My gentle splashings and slow careless snatchings yielded similar results — a lot of green amphibious bodies hopping away as I successfully caught clumps of mud-covered grass.

"You'll never catch anything like that," my grandmother called.

My brother and I stopped our tromping and stood erect. As we wiped mud, grass, and water on our shorts, we waited for our grandmother's scolding. Instead, she came toward us carrying cups made of thin rigid plastic.

"If you're going to catch frogs, you have to stay still in one place," she said. Then, demonstrating from the dry ground, she continued to explain. "Hold the cup from the bottom with one hand. Cup the other hand and make it ready to close in on top of the cup." As she explained and demonstrated this procedure, my grandfather came out with a grimy painter's bucket which he dipped in the drainage ditch, partially filling it with murky water.

"Here. Put them in here when you've caught them," he said.

Armed with plastic cups and their approval, my brother and I attempted once again to catch frogs.

In silence, I crept behind my first victim. Its head and eyes poked above the water while its body remained submerged in the swamp. In my left hand, I held the bottom of the cup and brought the open end of the cup behind the dark slick body of the frog. Parallel to the cup, I stiffened my palm and fingers in anticipation of my first capture of the day. Inching closer to the frog, I closed in on the frog.

"Now. Trap the frog as quick as you can," my grandmother whispered.

In one quick awkward movement, I slammed cup and hand together, only to come up empty.

"Try again," my grandmother coached. "But come from the sides."

Stepping closer to the frog with my best attempt at stealth, I brought the cup and my hand closer to the frog, flanking it on either side. With steady speed, I closed my right hand over the top of the cup.

"You catch anything?" my grandfather barked.

Moving a finger to the side, just wide enough to peek through my hand and into the cup, I saw the slimy body of a frog, throat pulsating in rapid movements as its dark left eye stared back at me.

"Yeah," I said as I marched over to the bucket, holding my cup high so my brother and grandparents could see. With the top of the cup covered by my right hand, I lowered the cup into the bucket and released my catch.

That afternoon, my grandparents stood on the lawn watching my brother and me make one muddy attempt after another to catch enough frogs to fill the bucket my grandfather brought out for us. By the time we had to clean up for dinner, the bottom of the bucket hopped with the life of slimy amphibious bodies piled on top of each other.

"Timmy," my grandmother said, peering into the bucket. "How many did you and Peter catch?"

"Twenty-six? I can't tell," I said. "They're moving too much."

"Good job," my grandmother said.

"I'm hungry," my brother said.

"Good," my grandfather barked. "It's time to get cleaned up for dinner."

"What're we having?" my brother said.

My grandfather locked eyes with my brother. "Chicken, green beans, and mashed potatoes. You gonna eat those?"

My brother nodded.

"Good," my grandfather said.

My grandfather grabbed the bucket and dumped a hopping waterfall of slime and mud into the swampy drainage ditch. My grandmother led my brother and me into the cabin, where we took a bath and changed into soft, floral scented pajamas. Sitting down to eat, my grandfather prayed for the meal. As we ate, my brother stabbed, prodded, and poked at his food, eventually eating every piece of baked chicken, green beans, and mashed potatoes. Maybe my brother had simply been hungry enough to finally eat what my grandparents were serving, or maybe they'd coaxed him just enough with a cleverly devised distraction.

To find out more about Timothy R. Baldwin
and his books, visit
www.indiesunited.net/timothy-baldwin

Colonist

By Aaron Gallagher

Morning, and the sunrise exploded vivid reds and yellows and oranges, each color more beautiful than the last. Philip lay on his bed, the last rising note of his alarm fading. He could tell even through the ultraviolet screen that the sky burned with beautiful colors. He thought the sky beautiful and felt it a shame he could not open the window to look. The sunlight, pouring unchecked through the depleted atmosphere, would cause melanomas. The pollution filtered the sunlight into the amazing lightshow, both beautiful and deadly. The chemicals in the air would scar his lungs in moments.

He rose smoothly from his bed, spent a few moments deep-bending and stretching to loosen his muscles. He padded into the front room of his tiny apartment, a tall and lean man, handsome enough, with a small fuzz of toast-brown hair perched atop his close-shorn skull. He drew a glass of water from the expensive filter and sipped it, looking into the front room.

The transparent display over the window that faced the city showed him the time, temperature, weather, pollen levels, traffic warnings, and radiation count. Philip sighed and got out the raincoat with the heavy lining. Lead, and coated with flexible Pyrex laminate. Guaranteed to keep his organs and sperm safe while he had to be out of doors.

"Not so bad, though," he didn't realize spoke out loud. "Could be worse. Pollen count could be higher." He had forgotten his nose filter once; mutated pollen had taken root in his left lung. An aggressive type of chrysanthemum had sprouted in the tissue. The hospital bill had been enormous, and eight months of extra pay had gone to whittling it down. He hadn't forgotten his filter since.

"Best be off," he said to himself. He talked to himself so often and for so long that he had lost his internal monologue. He broadcast most every thought. This had embarrassed him more than once.

He shrugged into the heavy coat. and slipped his feet into the matching boots. His own shoes were tucked into the inside pouch. He tugged the hood over his head and sealed the faceplate.

"Another day," he said. "Another credit."

Before he opened his door, he grabbed up a pen dangling on a string. On the back of his reinforced door hung a year-long calendar. Two hundred days had heavy black Xs through them.

"Sixteen left," he said. "Only sixteen."

October twenty-sixth. Sixteen days away. Only sixteen days.

"Sixteen," he said to himself. "Only sixteen. Sixteen."

He palm-locked the door behind him.

"Fifteen, when this one's done."

He trudged down the hall. Yellowed paint clung desperately to the concrete walls. The carpet had long ago ceased to be any color but brown. The nappy, threadbare old carpet felt spongy under his heavy boots.

"No wonder," he said. "No wonder this place is disintegrating."

He didn't even look at the elevator. For one thing, it would take forever to get up to sixty-seven, his floor. For another, it would likely be filled with joy-riders, young punks with glassy pupils and terrible posture. They waited until someone in a hurry got on. Then, if you were lucky, they keyed the elevator to stop at every floor just for a laugh. Or, if you were unlucky, they robbed and beat you. That had happened to Philip only once. He had never again tried to take the elevator. Philip prided himself on never making the same mistake twice.

He stopped at the door to the stairwell. Sixty-seven floors. Sixty-seven. He squared his shoulders and opened the door.

The primary advantage to suiting up before leaving his apartment was the filter kept out the smell. The half-full building had plenty of empty apartments in which to squat, but for some reason a whole army of displaced persons lived in the stairwell. Squatters. Figuratively, literally, and biologically.

"Why?" he asked himself, stepping carefully around the bodies and leavings. "Why? Apartments have plumbing, lots have beds… why here? Like animals, they are."

Philip stopped talking. It took a lot of effort and oxygen to walk down sixty-seven flights of stairs.

He would probably have moved by now, if he didn't ride home from the office with Mark Happard, a senior accountant. Mark had a hover-car cleared for seventy stories. He dropped Philip off on the roof every night. Philip had to walk down only three sets of stairs to get home. His life seemed filled with convenience.

"Whole life is downhill," he said. "Always downhill. Could be worse. Could always be worse."

Philip reached the door to the first floor of his apartment building. He paused as he usually did, to catch his breath. He hated to walk into the lobby breathing hard. He waited for his heart to settle into a nominally slower rhythm. He pushed open the door with its flaking green paint and crossed the dingy lobby. The abandoned wrecks of sofas and chairs huddled in the corners like refugees, soaked and charred from being alternately set on fire and doused. A gang of kids, bizarrely-dressed in neon and clear plastic, sat moodily waiting for the elevator to open.

They bristled variously with bats, pipes, and chains. The latest fashion in street crime appeared to be retro weaponry. Apparently, Philip reflected, it's passé to shoot someone to death; beating them is the nouveau style. He waved to one of the youths, a sneering boy named Hart. Hart, the son of one of the tenants on Philip's floor, fetched groceries for Philip. Hart did this gladly, and declined the tips Philip set aside for the boy. Hart stopped snarling long enough to wave jauntily back. He resumed his snarl before his coterie could call him out for the unforgivable sin of politeness.

Philip had worked out early why Hart refused tips. No matter the size of his order, Hart lugged it willingly to Philip's door. No matter the size of the order, Hart refused to accept tips.

It hadn't occurred to Philip right away that Hart wasn't purchasing the groceries. He made a hundred percent profit from his venture. Philip wondered if he should stop paying the boy, but he reconciled with the idea. He, Philip, paid full price for the groceries in good faith. The boy brought him the groceries. Therefore, Philip paid for what he received. Any further transactions were none of his business.

As he stepped out of the building into the searing yellow sunlight it occurred to Philip to wonder how many other tenants were sending the gangs for groceries. The boys might very well be the richest occupants of the entire tenement. Entrepreneurial spirit at work. They worked hard for the money, really, because the food centers were much further from the building than they really should be. Since the city began dying, life migrated to the center. Philip's building lay on the outskirts of the withering city.

There were papers in the street; old, ripped newspapers. They flopped listlessly in the breeze. Dried, desiccated, yellowed. Why was it always newspapers? That had to be some kind of cliché. There hadn't been a print newspaper for a hundred years, and yet the streets were still windblown with newspapers. The dirty streets were half-full of dead, damp leaves. It had rained in the night. Philip trudged to the bus stop, boots crunching dead leaves.

At the corner, he waited with eleven other suited people for the wheezing airbus. As he stepped on and dropped his change in the meter in turn with the others, he wondered where the leaves always came from.

"Aren't any trees here," he said. "Haven't been trees in the city for a long time."

An ancient woman looked up when he spoke. Her expensive safety gear was transparent. The cheap stuff, like his, was opaque. It did the job, but Philip was not the model of the fashionable urban dweller. At some point, the old woman had been able to purchase the top-of-the-line weather gear. Everyone else wore dark, drab, ordinary safety clothing. One wheezing young man in the back had none.

Her pink dress was faded with age, much like the owner. She clutched a small plastic purse in her hands, grimly. It was clear plastic, and showed a threadbare change purse, a handkerchief, and a nonlethal ceramic stun gun. The clear plastic was a giveaway. She worked in a large retail outlet. They demanded all personal belongings to be clear. The old woman must submit to x-rays entering and leaving, for she chose not to wear clear plastic clothing. Some dignity, rather than none. But the x-rays obviously couldn't be good for her.

A bulbous growth stemming from her hairline and drooping down covered her left eye completely. He saw the elderly thing had painted an eyebrow on it, so that both sides matched. Her lipstick blazed red, too harsh for her age. At her ears were tiny dots of silver, earrings that no doubt contained hearing aids.

"Poor dear," Philip said. "Poor, poor dear."

"I beg your pardon?" The matron asked him.

Philip had already taken a seat toward the middle of the bus and didn't hear her. She didn't pursue the matter. She stared ahead and counted the street signs.

Philip looked out the darkened windows at the city streaming past. Burned-out cars littered the sidewalks. Bodies lay in doorways. They passed a group of youths beating on one another with long poles. A smaller group of police officers watched them, not interfering. They would arrest the winners, perhaps. Or just pay off their bets with each other and finish their lunches.

Thirty minutes of stops and starts and Philip stood up to exit the bus. The autodriver slowed to a halt, and Philip stepped off the bus. He felt the patter of rain on his hood and felt thankful for the protection. When the pollution counts were really high, the quaint term 'acid rain' took on an entirely new and unpleasant meaning.

He looked to his left. The homeless man from the bus, braving the outdoors without protection gear, hunched and huddled to keep the water off his skinny arms. The water raised red welts where it touched him. Philip shook his head. The man would be damaged beyond repair by now and unable to emigrate, even supposing he could find the fee.

Philip approached the awning over the door of his office. In the heart of downtown, the Office of Emigration Administration represented to most of the surrounding buildings a pie-in-the-sky dream. Everyone who foresaw a future worth having wanted to get off the dying Earth, but less than a quarter of all applicants were genetically lucky enough.

Fully half of the applicants got flagged for health reasons stemming from living in the poisonous atmosphere of the city. Philip turned away dozens without ever meeting them: the first requirement for an application being a sound bill of health from an approved hospital.

In the lobby of the building, Philip began the series of

decontamination steps required to allow him into the bowels of the building. His garments were cleaned, his radiation levels checked, his toxicology screen needed to be performed, and he needed to put on his shoes. Getting into his office every morning took nearly an hour.

He stored his weather gear in a locker. He nodded to the guards standing watch over the door, and went to the elevator.

Being in an energy economy, he waited for a small crowd to build before pressing 'up'. No sense wasting electricity for just him.

He and seven other workers, as well as one repeat applicant, stepped into the ancient box, and waited patiently for the squeaking cables to draw them up.

Philip's office, on the seventeenth floor, also happened to be the stop for the car's non-employee rider. Philip held open the door for Mister Alfred P. Sidcup.

Tall, gangly, and pale beyond pale, Mr. Sidcup applied for emigrant status every two weeks. He paid for the battery of tests, he sat patiently through the needles and the questions and the probes, and listened with no discernible reaction to the news that his cancers had not yet receded enough for him to attain flight clearance.

Alfred Sidcup was rich, moderately. That in and of itself not being enough to secure him a ride off the planet, he set about the task of slowly bankrupting himself in order to qualify. Sidcup Industries, Inc, mass-produced a line of home tests for cancer. People across the globe tested themselves regularly for one of a thousand varieties of cancer, most of which were treatable, if caught early.

When the doctors employed by Sidcup managed to invent a truly cheap testing apparatus, most of the world's cancer statistics began plummeting. A couple varieties, skin, pancreas, lung, and brain, were as-yet uncured. The death rates on those were near 100%. All the others were treatable if caught early.

Sidcup Industries ensured that all cancers could be caught early, and for comparatively cheap.

The irony of Alfred Sidcup discovering his own cancers in the preliminary test phase of his own products did not escape either Sidcup or Philip.

Philip led the way to his office. Alfred, with a wave, peeled off down a corridor toward the medical offices. Philip crossed his tiny cubical and sat at his desk. In the cubby behind his desk, his ancient coffee maker burbled quietly.

Philip didn't have a secretary, but he did have a devoted following of coffee drinkers in his office. Since the Administration operated around the clock, someone always had a pot brewing. Since Philip had supplied the coffee maker, he always got the lion's share of the fresh coffee. Other coffee makers existed, but his was the only pressure-style coffee maker any of them had ever seen. The coffee his ancient machine produced tasted better than anything to be had from the modern plastic hot-pots.

On Philip's desk a stack of papers waited. The latest lists of accepted and rejected candidates. As he had been doing for nearly a year, he checked for his own name.

There it was, in black and white. Number seven hundred twenty-two: Kay, Philip D. Estimated launch date: October twenty-sixth.

He smiled with happiness, a warm glow suffusing his body. He always feared the list. He submitted to the medicals every two weeks, followed his protocols exactly, took his vitamin boosters, and never left his house or office without being completely sealed into his safety gear, but he still feared the list.

"Only for another sixteen, old boy," he said to himself. "Only for another fifteen days, as soon as this one is over."

Philip Kay. Mid-level administrator for the Office of Emigration Administration, scheduled for launch. He would be bustled into a suit, hustled onto a pad, strapped into a seat, and launched from Earth into orbit. He would spend a day headed for Luna Station, and from there to the colony on Mars.

Most of the first emigrants had been vital in one area or another. Medical, construction, scientific, piloting, and exploration fields had been granted protected status. After those had filled, other criterion had been established. Criterion starting with health and enveloping all areas of performance. You didn't need a critical trade to be selected. Colonies needed strong backs as well as strong minds. You did, however, need to pass the physical, mental, and emotional qualifying tests. Anyone unable to withstand the first flight off Earth, for instance, was disqualified. No sense spending billions of credits to launch corpses. Or mental defectives. Or emotionally unstable potential psychopaths. Space began to fill up with the most desirable of humanity. The dregs were left to survive or not on Earth.

He had been extremely fortunate. Although he served as a paper-pusher, his degree happened to be in mathematics, with a specialization in astrophysics. His had been the last class to graduate from Berkeley before the college system had collapsed, reemerging three years later as a glorified trade school cum daycare center.

Philip could perform advanced calculations without resorting to his fingers, and he could do a surprising number of correlated feats as well. His education, however, wasn't as much use on Earth as it had been in years past. He had been lucky to find work in the office. Lucky to have been single. Lucky to have been able to survive on the pittance he made.

In all his years since college, Philip had never met a woman with whom he felt comfortable. He had supposed that he would die alone, in his apartment, probably from some kind of environmental cause.

One slow afternoon, for fun, the crowds in his office decided to all take the preliminary mental exams. Only fifteen of the thirty-seven people in Philip's office had passed the exams. Of those fifteen, only thirteen had passed the emotional screening.

Of those thirteen, only six passed the physical.

Of those six, only Philip had declined to apply for emigration status.

He had decided that Earth was his home, for better or worse, and that he was not up to a life on the frontier.

A visit from the head of Administration changed his mind. In no uncertain terms the man, an aging giant named Richards, had put a fatherly arm on Philip's shoulder and explained what a coup it would be for the Administration to send some of its people Up.

They guaranteed him a living space and a job. His skills with the administration of a large-scale project would come in handy, and even if he had only been a ditch-digger, he was still qualified to teach Astrophysics. There was a need. A Call. And he had been requested.

Finally, Philip had allowed himself to be persuaded. And once he had accepted his slot, he discovered a long-dormant emotion hiding within his unassuming frame.

Hope.

In the leading frontier of man's future, he would have a place. He would have a spot. He would be valuable. No more rotting apartment buildings. No more gangs of toughs waiting to either rob him or steal groceries for him. No lonely life.

No lonely life.

He would be among people whose existence had been validated by all the tests man could devise to assure itself of someone's basic worth to the race.

Philip began the day's work by reading over the newly-accepted applications from the last twelve hours. Part of his job required him to contact the accepted candidates and explain the process, time frames, and help them settle last-minute details.

There were eight of them. He felt a tiny chill rush up his spine as he realized that here in his hands were eight more people that would be locked into blast chairs on that shuttle with him.

He rifled the papers. He stopped at the third sheet of flimsy. His breath stuttered. It was <u>her</u>.

Alexandra Aderline.

He re-read it. Incorrect. Her name wasn't Aderline any longer. She had married.

Alexandra Aderline-Carmichael.

He scanned the sheet. She was a lottery winner. She had bought passage off Earth. It was possible, of course. A seat could be had for a measly million credits. It was simple and it cut down on bribe attempts. Provided you passed the medicals, of course, a ticket could be purchased.

He looked over her medical report. It all looked fine. A tiny murmur, nothing really worrisome. She had been passed, provisionally. They implanted a recorder, and in a couple weeks would remove it and check again.

Alexandra Aderline. His heart sank. Carmichael. Married. He shook his head. Too good to be true, he supposed.

He looked through the rest of the sheets, uninterested in them. He sorted them into the file, and set about his day's work. His eyes stole again and again to the file cabinet where her picture lay waiting for him to break and take it out again, which he would.

Alexandra Aderline.

PART II

In the after-lunch session, Philip sat against the wall of the stage area. The moldering curtains hid him from sight. He turned the page of the book in his lap and continued reading. He should be in History Two, but he found the class to be a bore, and depressing, since all their history lessons ultimately ended with 'and then the bombs dropped, and people began to flee the Earth, except for the too stupid, or too twisted genetically, or just sub-par in a measurable way.'

He didn't have many friends among the small set of youths who made up what would turn out to be the last class graduating from their school. Philip preferred quiet to noise, solitude to group activities, and study alone to classrooms. The few teachers dedicated to actually trying to instruct the students left Philip alone because he never troubled them. He did the work, he passed the tests, and if his performances were unremarkable, at least he wasn't roving the streets in ever-more common gangs of feral children intent on vandalism and thievery.

His attentions were largely taken by a girl in his second period literature class. Her auburn hair and blue eyes, too big for her delicately-constructed features, captivated him in ways that he could only just fathom. Of course he had, like all the other children, begrudgingly sat through the required reproductive seminars, and submitted to the regularly-scheduled inoculations that the schools administered to stem the tide of unwanted pregnancies, if not venereal disease. Most of his classmates were paired, or pairing. They were all over seventeen, weren't they? None of them were strangers to the act itself, or the process of finding places to perform it. Except for Philip. He knew what he should be doing, and how. He simply didn't have the courage to ask her.

He would have, honestly, if he hadn't discovered his intended in a warm and sticky embrace with another boy, hiding behind the curtains of the decaying stage in the theater.

He did not understand that his subconscious, driven by the sight of his crush naked and writhing, drew him again and again to this place. He thought he sought solitary and peace. His internal drives knew better. He wanted those things, true, but he wouldn't be put out if he discovered her here again. The one flash of her he had in his mind, back arched, breasts drawn taut, hair cascading backward, errant strands glued to her skin with sweat, called to him in his dreams.

He had never spoken to her.

Philip didn't know what he should say. Sorry I caught you… what? What does one say to a young lady who… well… who wasn't exactly a candidate for lady-hood, truth be told. Tell her he thought she was pretty? Ask her to a dance? Ask her to do it with <u>him</u> in the theater?

Cold sweat covered his brow every time he considered this last notion.

Philip lusted after her for a year. He never took another class with her. The following year he graduated. She graduated. A single semester later, the prestigious school shut down, never to reopen again as an institution of truly higher learning again. More importantly to Philip, he never saw her again.

PART III

Philip reopened the drawer, and took her flimsy from the folder again. A thought had occurred. He scanned her sheet. Married, at nineteen. He didn't remember the name of her boyfriend from school, but the last name rang a bell. He smiled. She married her college sweetheart. She married her college sweetheart. She hadn't been having a fling. She'd been in love.

He smiled wider. It almost made it okay, finding that out. Almost made the years of wistful wonder worth it. He had pined for her, but she had taken what she wanted. He had kept his desire to himself, she had shared hers and made it into a life.

He shook his head, almost paternally. He knew in his heart she probably wasn't the <u>one</u> for him. Most of the time, the people that get away aren't that special. It's the not knowing that tears us open, makes us bleed hope. Still, she had come to him in dreams off and on in the ten years since leaving school.

He dismissed his notions and scanned the rest of the information in her file. Husband... husband... there. Husband named Frank. Frank Carmichael.

Philip didn't remember the boy and that made sense. He wouldn't have wanted to remember. Aside from catching them together, Philip had made a habit of never seeing the boy again. He set her sheet on the desk and went to his files again.

He found Carmichael, Frank C. The sheet was in his 'in' box, awaiting his approval or rejection. It would be a rejection. Listed under reasons, he discovered a heart condition. Serious enough to warrant rejecting him. His heart could stop during launch, probability seventieth percentile. The gee forces of a chemical rocket were extreme. Alternately, the months in free-fall could be just as deadly. He could develop an arrhythmia and suffer cardiac arrest on the trip. Transport tubes were stripped-down ships; they carried fuel and food for the trip, and nothing else. They were bare-bones ships, into which every possible able body would be crammed. It was a small price to pay for life among the stars, or a chance at a newer, healthier life among the colonies.

Frank Carmichael's incipient heart condition put him in a ninetieth percentile group for likely heart attack in free-fall. The cutoff ruled by the congressional edicts placed the line at ten percent or less for approval.

Frank Carmichael had never stood a chance.

Philip sighed.

He went back to the accepted file cabinet and searched. Momentarily, he pulled his own acceptance sheet out and was examining it.

Alexandra Aderline.

He could still remember her eyes. Her cheekbones. He found himself imagining the look on her face as she found out her husband wouldn't be accompanying her. The tears. The arguments. He would want her to go, but not really. She wouldn't want to go, but not really. They would either part friends or enemies. They would stay lovers, or stay resentfully sullen, and angry, and eventually break apart, devolving into hatred. Philip's heart thumped painfully at the idea of her eyes filled with tears, brimming and spilling over.

He shook his head, clearing away the vision from his sight, now over-bright and color-sharpened.

He played around for a moment with his desk terminal and produced a new acceptance sheet. It had all of his official marks on it, the acceptance numbers from the Board. It was a perfectly-reproduced copy of his acceptance sheet… with Frank Carmichael's name and vital statistics, aside from the minor correction about his heart. Carmichael now had Philip's medical history, including the minor hearing loss in his left ear, and his perfect EKG readouts, all three of them.

He dialed their listed house number.

After a moment there came a click and a voice. The same voice that had haunted his adolescent dreams.

"Yes? Hello?"

"Alex-" Philip cleared his throat. Embarrassment? Shyness? He was a grown man, for God's sake, and she was a married woman. She wouldn't even remember him, most likely. He tried again. "Alexandra Aderline-Carmichael?"

"This is she," said his dream-girl's voice. "Who's calling?"

"My name is-is Philip Kay, ma'am. I'm with the Emigration Bureau."

He closed his eyes as she caught her breath. She was afraid of him now, afraid that he would be breaking her heart. He smiled. He didn't have to do that. He would likely be fired for what he was about to do, but at least he wouldn't be breaking her heart. He didn't think he could bear the pain of that betrayal. To crush this woman's hopes. She would never know him, never know how he had felt, never understand why he was now jeopardizing his future, and throwing away his potential. But at least he didn't have to break her heart. On the contrary, he was giving her a chance for happiness that he fervently hoped would make her smile, maybe even dance.

"Is-is everything… I mean…" Alexandra didn't finish her sentence. The silence crushed Philip. He couldn't keep her in suspense, his dream-girl. His crush. His love. His only love, aside from the idea of a new start. A new life.

"Ma'am, I assure you, everything is perfectly fine. Tell me, have you any plans that extend beyond the next two weeks? Because I'm afraid you'll have to cancel them."

"I-I don't… wait. Wait. Are you… are you telling me…?"

"I am. Congratulations, Mrs. Carmichael. You've been selected to become a colonist. I'm exceedingly happy for you, truly I am."

"Oh, that's wonderful! Frank!" Alexandra yelled, covering the mouthpiece inadequately. "Frank! It's the Bureau! They-"

She broke off, addressed Philip again.

"But… but what about… I mean…"

"Is your husband at home, Mrs. Carmichael? Because it will save me a call if he is. Will you tell your husband that he has been accepted?"

Alexandra squealed. "Oh, thank you! Thank you, sir! Thank you!"

Philip smiled. He had made her very happy. He enjoyed the warm glow. It would make everything worth it. Knowing that. Besides, there was a chance her husband would survive. Stranger things had happened. There were no medical personnel on the flight, but they did heavily sedate the passengers. Safer for them. Sedated passengers rarely threw up or became unruly. The sedation might compensate for Frank's heart defect and allow him to reach the colony safely. Philip hoped so.

"Thank you, thank you!" Alexandra gushed. "Thank you so

very much!"

"You're quite welcome, ma'am," Philip said again. "Quite welcome."

A new voice now, in the background. Deeper, and just as excited. Frank.

"What's this, honey? We made it?"

"We made it, Frank! We made it! We're shipping out!"

A rustling noise, and Frank's voice came to Philip.

"Thank you, sir. We're grateful for your call."

"My pleasure, Mr. Carmichael. My job, but also my pleasure. These calls are my favorite part of the day. Have you a pen? I will need to give you some information."

"Certainly, certainly. Hold on a moment."

Philip poured himself a cup of coffee while he waited. Frank came back on the line.

"All right, Mr. Carmichael. Write these numbers down; they're your acceptance numbers. You'll be asked for them and your identification at the boarding gate."

Philip read off the numbers, double and treble-checking them against Frank's versions to make sure there were no mistakes.

"Excellent. Now, as you know, the next launch date is in sixteen days. You'll need to contact a Launch Attorney, they'll help you settle your estate here on Earth. Let me give you the hotline number."

"Of course." Frank scribbled the numbers down.

"Now, you're not allowed any luggage of any kind, as you certainly know. Minimal weight standards. You'll be given room, board, clothing, and food upon arrival at Luna Base."

"We can't take anything? What about pictures, letters from our families-"

"I'm sorry, Mr. Carmichael. Nothing at all. You may digitize your photos and send them to your email, but you cannot take any hard copies. You'll be searched before takeoff, both pat-down, cavity, and deep-scan searches. Your clothing will be confiscated, and you'll be issued a ship coverall. Your heads will be shaved. In fact, all of your body hair will be removed via electrolysis."

"That can't be a weight requirement," Frank said.

"Not at all, sir.It's a health requirement. They remove all your body hair. It keeps parasites down. They only have what they import up there, ha ha, and they have to be very careful and incredibly strict about what people take with them. You'll be getting a visit from a messenger around two days before launch, he'll have your immuno-boosters and all the necessary shots you'll need. There will be a number of them. You're required by law to submit."

"To a messenger?"

"Yes, sir. They're medically-trained and bonded."

"Oh, I see."

"Yes, sir. I think that's everything."

"You've been very helpful, Mister..." Frank paused. "I'm sorry, I don't know your name?"

"It's Kay, Mr. Carmichael. Philip Kay."

"Of course. Thank you very much, Mr. Kay. You're a welcome bearer of wonderful news. We appreciate it so very much."

Philip closed his eyes.

"I'm sure, sir. Good luck, have a safe flight."

"Thank you very much."

"And Mr. Carmichael?" Philip said.

"Sir?"

"Congratulations, and make the best of your chance, sir. Make good use of your new opportunity."

"I intend to, Mr. Kay. We intend to."

"Good-bye, Mr. Carmichael."

"Thank you, and good-bye, sir." Frank hung up the phone.

Philip hung up the phone and leaned back in his creaky

chair. The creaky chair in the tiny office in the run-down building in the rotting city in a desolate state in a shredded country on a dying world.

The chair he very suddenly would not be leaving behind in sixteen days, unless they fired him.

They wouldn't catch his bit of tomfoolery with the paperwork. No one checked up on Philip. He was the official keeper of the records. His was the final word. He wouldn't change any of the paperwork that hung in his office, and he wouldn't have to change anything else. He couldn't just slip himself onto the ship, though. They would know something was up when they came in one over the headcount. The weight of the ship had to be calculated precisely. So he would have to skip work that day. Maybe he'd go watch the launch. Then he would come into work the day after. It should be an interesting day.

He worked diligently until five o'clock. Mark Happard strolled in at five, helped himself to coffee, and slumped in Philip's one guest chair.

"You ready to go home, Kay?" He sipped noisily. Philip smiled.

"Good old home," Philip said. "Yes, I'm ready. Let me get my coat."

Philip stood up, gathered his things, dropped the day's stack of accepted into the file, and followed Happard to the roof.

Soon, he stood on the roof of his apartment building. He walked down the few flights to his apartment. He let himself in, locked the door behind him, and hung up his weather gear. No telling what it would be like tomorrow, yet. He smiled. It was a big day. He should celebrate.

He rang down to Hart's apartment, and asked Hart's aging mother to send the boy round.

"I'd like him to pick up some groceries for me."

"I'll tell 'im," the old woman said.

Soon, Hart knocked on the door. Philip checked the monitor. He liked Hart and knew him, but better safe than sorry, right? The boy was alone, however.

Philip opened the door. The boy slouched moodily against the frame, an unlit cigarette dangling from his mouth.

"What can I getcha, Mistah Kay?"

"I'd like a bottle of champagne, please, and a chicken breast. Any fresh vegetables you can put hands on."

The boy whistled, no mean feat around a cigarette.

"That's a lotta good stuff, Mistah Kay."

"I know, Hart. But I'm in a good mood, and I feel like celebrating. How much do you suppose it'll be?"

"Oh..." he figured, rolling his eyes upward. "Prolly be around seventy. Maybe eighty."

Philip nodded. He drew out his wallet and took a hundred credits from it. He handed it to the boy. "Whatever you think, Hart. And keep the change."

The boy's eyebrows popped up.

"Thanks, Mistah Kay. Thanks a lot."

"My pleasure."

"Did you get some good news, or what?" The boy asked.

Philips smiled. "I did, actually. I did." He nodded. "Please be quick as you can. I'm hungry."

"Sure thing, Mistah Kay. See you soon."

"I'll be here," Philip said. He closed the door after the boy, and grinned at the calendar on the back of his door. The board read 'Time left to departure: fifteen days.' He swiped a hand through the writing. The board now read: "Time left."

Philip picked up the marker and scribbled a note after the words. He let the marker drop on its string, and he walked into his small apartment to find something to do.

Behind him the board read: "Time left- all of it."

The End

To find out more about Aaron S Gallagher
and his books, visit
www.indiesunited.net/aaron-gallagher

Everyone's Gone to the Moon

By D. Krauss

About a week after Neil Armstrong came back from the moon, everybody went there. Everybody. Except me.

Rather unfair because I'd always wanted to go. When I was a kid, a little kid, one of my favorite picture books was *You Will Go to the Moon.* It showed a kid on the cover looking at the moon through a telescope and had all these neat illustrations of the kid and his dad getting ready to go to the moon base, although, now that I think about it, there was something a little sinister about the way all those grown men in space suits hovered around the little boy. I was entranced because being a space man would be cool, just not with my dad. And not back in the early 60s, when the moon was nothing but rock and dust; later, say in the 80s, when there was an actual moon base and a daily shuttle back and forth like in the book so I'd be home for dinner.

But when Neil stepped off the ladder onto a moon made of nothing but rocks and dust everybody fell into moon thrall and got hootin' and hollerin' and carrying on and at some point all looked at each other and said, "Let's go!" So they did. Hook. Crook, slapped together rocket ships, jet propelled sailboats, several banks of oars, I don't know. But they went. See, the whole world was in the grip of good ole American "can do!" spirit. If some sody-cracker freckled-faced white boy corn farmer can get to the moon, why can't we? It's sort of like when you hear about a great party: you just gotta go.

I understood that. The night of the moon landing, I was out in my backyard with some crappy Montgomery Wards telescope my dad had bothered to get for my 14th birthday a couple of months previous (complaining the whole time about how much it cost, the cheapass) and I swore, swore, I could see Mike Collins circling the earth in the command ship. Of course I couldn't. That was simple imagination. But what a powerful thing simple imagination can be. It caused a worldwide population transfer.

The cities on the moon are now so big I can see them without my crappy telescope. Yes, I still have it. It's not like there's a bunch of other telescopes lying around for the taking. The few times a year I manage to get to town and rummage through the five-and-dime, all I've ever found were even crappier telescopes, Japanese-made toys of plastic and overlapping cardboard cylinders that you pulled or pushed for focus. Compared to them, mine is the Palomar observatory. Which, I guess, is still there. Probably all rusted and overgrown, but there.

Whenever the moon is full and so bright that using the telescope smarts the eyes, I pull a mattress out on the lawn and lay back and watch the moon cities glow and sparkle and slowly cover a little bit more of the seas and craters and mountains, changing the topography of the moon so that I no longer recognize the old features. The Man in the Moon is gone, but there's certainly a lot of men on the moon. And women. And kids. Otherwise, how are things getting built? It's taken the cities about fifty years to reach their current sizes and it will probably be another fifty before their borders touch each other, if they ever do. Humans may have gone to the moon but they're still humans and I have no doubt they brought their irritations along with them. I've never seen any evidence of moon wars, no gigantic dust or mushroom clouds roiling over the cities, but I have to think there's conflict. We are who we are.

I wonder what's happened to all the nuke missiles and bombs left here on Earth? All rusted and overgrown, I suppose.

I haven't heard from anybody who went to the moon. I haven't heard from anybody at all anywhere, so I don't know what happened, but I can guess. When the euphoria finally dissipated, everybody up there looked around and went, "Man, sure a lot of nothing." No fertile fields, no rivers, no cattle. Not even a Piggly Wiggly. So they took apart everything they brought with them and got to work but limited resources, ya know? Became dog eat dog, or people eating people, which is why I'd hesitate if moon men showed up now offering me a ride because I must look like a prize beef cow. An old one, but with a lot more meat on me then they must have, what with zero gravity and zero hamburgers — beef ones, that is. The strong ate the weak and the survivors were tough and ruthless and resourceful and, presto chango, cities on the moon. I noticed them about ten years ago. Took awhile before they got big enough for me to pick them up on my crappy telescope. Since then, they've really taken off.

I wonder how they're doing it? It's not like there's a hardware store at the corner of Tycho Crater and Hadley Rill. The closest hardware store to me is in Enterprise and it takes me a day to get there and most everything in it is now rusted and overgrown or warped and moldy so, imagine. I'm guessing they found a lot more stuff on the moon than we all knew at the time: water and metals and chemicals of some kind or another. We thought it was all silicon dust and iron fragments of meteors, nothing else. Surprise, surprise, surprise.

I wonder if I'm the only human left who gets that reference.

No, Dad would get it. I am more than sure he's still alive, one of the tough and ruthless and resourceful who ate the weak and then became a fine citizen of whatever moon city he's in. Probably lionized as one of the Grand Old Men of the Great

Moon Launch, I'll bet. Fooled them, fooled everybody, just like here. He's probably got a chain of moon bars selling illegal hooch made out of moon dust or something, my brother helping. Gotta admit, Dad was a guy for getting things done. I mean, the very moment Neil and Buzz raised the flag on Tranquility Base, Dad grabbed a flashlight and went right out to the shed and started throwing together sheet metal and old wall board and kerosene and cases of C-Rations from Dubya Dubya Too he'd collected (stole) from the Army. I followed him because I thought he was going to mess with my crappy telescope still up and pointing at the moon. "What are you doing?" I asked.

Flashlight in my eyes. "What's it look like I'm doing?"

"Making a mess?"

He then cursed me out for about five minutes, standard fare, and from that I gleaned he was building a moon ship. "A moon ship," was my somewhat incredulous response.

"Yeah, smart ass, a moon ship!" And he threw a C-rat at me, which I expected and easily ducked. Standard fare.

"What are you going to do with a moon ship?"

"What the hell do you think? Go to the moon!" And he looked at me like I was an idiot.

"Can I come?" my brother squeaked.

"Sure!" Dad said, then snake-eyed me, "You can't."

I looked at them like they were both idiots and then went inside and fell asleep in front of the TV watching Walter Cronkite gush about Buzz and Neil cavorting on the moon. The next morning, Dad and my brother took off. I stood in the yard next to the wash house as the two of them threw some duffel bags filled with crap into the hold of this contraption he'd built and then got inside and closed it down with one of those big iron wheels you see in submarine movies. "Are you kidding me?" I called.

No.

With a roar that blew me across the yard and into the side of the house hard enough to break one of my toes, they blasted off. I was too stunned to watch the entire thing, but managed to look up in enough time to see their bright white Roman candle of a moon ship disappear into the clouds. "Are you kidding me?" I whispered.

The toe never healed right and I still walk with a hitch. The burns scarred over and restricted my left hand somewhat, but I'm all right. Physical injuries aren't really a problem, I've discovered. Sling 'em or band-aid 'em and slather on as much Unguentine as I dare 'cause I'm down to my last case, and I end up all right. It's illness that scares me. Don't have to worry about the flu; no one to catch it from, but there's other things. I had some real bad lung thing going about the time I turned twenty, or thereabouts (I've lost track of years and days so I'm just guessing). I injected myself with penicillin I took out of the Fort Rucker emergency room and got even sicker, thought I was gonna die. Must have gone bad or something. I recovered, obviously, but I'm real careful about infections and cuts and rusty nails and things like that because even the hydrogen peroxide has gone flat.

What do you expect after fifty years? Thereabouts.

The three or four days after Dad left, I saw other launches, neighbors piling into their own sheet metal contraptions and lighting off whatever fuel they'd mixed, the roar of the engines signaling me and I'd limp out to the front porch and follow their contrails arcing across the sky. Three or four a day. We've got big clear skies here in Alabama and I saw launches from as far away as Enterprise, I'm sure. And then there were no more.

I tried calling people first. I'd pick up the phone and listen to see if anyone was on the party line. "Hello? Hello?" but no one responded so I dialed Mom's number in New Jersey, giggling because Dad would explode when the long-distance bill came in, but no one answered. I called uncles and aunts there and in Texas and tried all my friends in Goodman and New Brockton and Fort Rucker but nothing. I left the phone off the hook expecting any second for some old biddy to screech, "Hang up, you've got the line blocked!" like they always did when they wanted to call some other biddy and gossip but that never happened. Phone's still off the hook. Still silent.

I feasted off everything in the freezer and refrigerator, eating up all the ice cream in one night and deliberately leaving the cartons out on the screened-in porch to teach Dad a lesson but all I got for that was wolf rats all over the table so I cleaned up and burned it all. Dad would have been proud. When I was down to six or seven cans of Campbell's Tomato Soup, I rode my bike over to the neighbors and broke in and took their cans. Helluva job hauling all that over on my bike handles. We only have two neighbors within two miles so I hit Bark's Store and then Goodman and then it was too far on bike so I taught myself to drive Dad's truck, rearranging the front grill and side panels slamming into things and giggling the whole time about how mad he'd be. Took me a bit to get the hang of it, taking corners and stuff but, once I did, I had fun.

Road trips!

I went to Opp and Elba and Montgomery, and then Atlanta. New York City, wow. I took all this jewelry out of Macy's and ran naked down the middle of Broadway because the whole place was nothing but porno posters. Got stuck there because it snowed and had to wait for spring. Man. New York City is nothing but porno and rats. I went home after that. Nothing else to see.

No one else to see.

The truck has long since died and so has every other car and gas station in the world. My bike still works well enough, three speeds, but tires are a constant problem and besides, I don't really have anywhere to go. Library in Fort Rucker, that's about it, and I am a real stickler for borrowing and returning, even though it takes me a day to get there and a day back. I've pretty much read everything in there that interested me, Ray Bradbury and Robert Heinlein and Mark Twain but I read them over and over. What else is there to do?

I don't have any electricity. Power died years ago and I have no idea how to fix it. I spent a couple of weeks reading books and walking around the power plant in Enterprise but some things are beyond me. Dad would have been able to figure it out. He was always good at stuff like that. So was my brother. I wasn't. I'd look at a hammer and nail, baffled. Guess that's why he left me. What use am I?

What use?

I eat well. Pioneer well. I hunt with bow and arrow, which I had always been pretty good with. I have Dad's rifles and shotgun and pistols and ammo but I keep all that clean and dry and ready in case the moon men attack. Dad reloaded his own shells and I have figured out how to do that but I don't know how long powder and primer can last so, no, save it for the moon men. I can stalk a deer or wild pig well enough with the arrows and I have lots of arrows because Dad had a lot of them, even fletched his own. I've learned how to do that, too, so there, Dad. I was always good in the garden and I grow corn and tomatoes and I have chickens, and there's always squirrels and opossum although I don't really like them.

I have a well.

I'm good.

I'm good.

Until yesterday.

I was sitting in a metal chair in the middle of the driveway looking across the road at a big ole pasture where the MacDonald's across the street kept a few cows before the Great Moon Launch. I was hoping a wild cow would come out of the woods and up to the fence like they used to because a hamburger would be nice when a UFO flew right over top the house and across the front yard and then right in front of me, hovering a few feet off my head. "Hello," it said in a girl's voice.

I wasn't really sure what to do, shoot it with an arrow or run screaming, so I said, "Hello," back.

"What's your name?" the girl Martian asked.

Figured it was a Martian, anyway. Thing looked weird, like a cross between a helicopter and a Frisbee, little blades arranged around its circular body and beating the air to hold it in place, lights glowing all over and what had to be a camera right in my face. Hadn't lasered me or shot me with a bee gun like in *The Martian Chronicles* so I decided to play along. "Butch."

"That's not a name," the Martian girl said, "That's a nickname."

"It's the last name I remember. What's yours?"

"Luna."

And then I knew. Not a Martian. "You're from the moon," I said.

"Well, yeah." Said like every teenage girl I had ever met back when there were teenage girls. You could almost hear her eyes roll. "We all are."

"I'm not." I pointed behind me. "I live here."

"Huh?" The helicopter Frisbee actually jumped a bit, like a startled teenage girl. "You don't live here. No one lives here."

"I do."

"Oh, stop," and she was giggling and I was in love. "How can you live on Earth? There's too many plants."

"How can you live on the moon? There's no plants."

"Of course there's plants, silly. In the hydro gardens."

I'd read something like that in a Clifford Simak book, I think, so I didn't say anything.

"How'd you get here?" Luna asked.

"I never left."

The Frisbee almost flipped over like she fell out of a chair or something. "What?? What!!" The Frisbee zoomed up close to my face and I did go over, landing with a metal clatter on the gravel as the Frisbee followed me and the camera was six inches away from my face, hovering, and I figured I was dead. "Did you… did you get left behind?" Luna sounded like she was crying.

"Yes. By my dad."

The Frisbee went crazy, flipping here and there as Luna babbled about all the work she'd done on this project and she was going to get an 'A' (so schools haven't changed much) but then she saw me and figured Simpson (or some name like that) was messing with her and she was gonna kill him and this just can't be real then the Frisbee stopped and drifted and looked right down at me and I braced for a bee gun. "I've got to tell someone!" she said all breathless and, just like that, the Frisbee zoomed up and away and gone.

I waited a few minutes, checking myself for bees, and then got up and went into the house and retrieved the guns and the ammo and made barricades and here I am, waiting for a moon man attack. Was bound to happen. We are who we are.

So it looks like I will go to the moon, anyway.

But not without a fight.

To find out more about D. Krauss
and his books, visit
www.indiesunited.net/d-krauss

Flight or Fight

by T. Gamache

She sat in the her assigned seat and waited patiently for the plane to take off. As new passenger after new passenger walked by, she prayed a silent prayer to a deity she didn't believe in that no one would sit next to her. But he did. He climbed over her, making her feel incredibly uncomfortable, for no man should walk his privates in front of a woman's face. But this man was a normal pig.

They sat in silence as the plane took off and finally reached altitude, when the pain began. The man broke the silence.

"Whatcha' reading?" he asked without her solicitation. He smelled of bacon, Diet Pepsi, and infidelity. She couldn't stand his voice or his face and she sure as shit wasn't going to entertain this animal for long.

"Just a boring article," she responded with a monotone and proceeded to put on her noise-cancelling headphones and escape into the Mozart. The man gave some type on snide remark that she missed as the opening notes of "The Marriage of Figaro" sent her into a space where only her memories could hurt her.

This flight wasn't supposed to be like this. She was supposed to have taken care of everything last night. But here she was, stuck in this inner turmoil with nothing but her thoughts. Why was she made like this? Her life had been anything but fair. It had been a struggle since she was fourteen and here she was, almost forty, and it wasn't getting any easier. The jobs and come and gone. Mostly gone, as was the same with her relationships. She couldn't manage to hold onto anyone before things inevitably got weird. But now, she had to figure out a way to keep her shit together log enough to land this next job. It was crucial. It was potentially her last chance. The bills were more than piling up and debt collectors and car repo guy were on a first name basis with her. This was her break. She would get the job, change locations (again), and finally see some daylight. She was more than qualified, and the job came with a car and a condo she could stay until the paychecks afforded her the luxury of having her own place.

But the pain. That was going to be the issue. The pain and the burning. It was not going to go away. Not before the interview. And then it was going to be over. No job and no future. Which is why she also packed the pistol. She would end it all in her hotel room if her illness prevented her from her life again. She had lived with it long enough and it was time for it to be over.

The man motioned to her that he needed to use the bathroom and the seat dance happened all over again. She would have gotten up and let him pass, but he made sure to not let that be an option. His disgusting belly touched her cheek as he went by and she really thought she was going to vomit. No amount of Mozart was going to erase that.

Then her mind started to wander. And this was never good. Why are there men like that in the world? What do they think is going to happen? If I come close enough to you, you're going just want to rip my clothes off and do me in the seat while the stewardess cleans up my plastic cup of Ginger Ale? Maybe. Maybe that is what he wants. And if this is potentially going to be my last flight, maybe I should let him. Maybe I should walk back there and let him have his ease with me in the bathroom. Pig. She had never been so disgusted.

With that, she got up and made her way to the back of the

plane. There was only one working bathroom and she knew he had to be in it. As the luck of the world was smiling on her that morning, there was no one sitting in the back row and no one waiting for the bathroom.

The door opened and they made eye contact. He smiled at her and she returned the gesture.

She pushed him back into the bathroom and locked the door behind her. He obviously was not expecting this and lost his footing a little. That worked well for her as she started to kiss him to keep him from talking. His hands quickly found their way around her body and he was obviously letting himself enjoy this. She wondered what was going through his mind at that moment. Was he the luckiest man in the world or what? Soon to be the newest member of the mile high club? Her hand started to rub his chest until she could feel his heart thumbing through his shirt. She could smell it too. It was a heart that had been abused by beer and bar food, but it was still pumping hard.

She slid her hand under his shirt and before he could say a word her fingers had penetrated skin through his rib cage and she was up to her wrist in his flesh. Her hand deftly found the heart muscle and grabbed it and completely ripped it from its normal place in his body. She pulled it back through his body and he quivered as he breathed his last. The muscle was tasty enough and she knew right there that the pain and burning would be at bay for at least another couple of weeks. She had fed. She had fulfilled her desires. She would get the job.

She washed her hands, walked back to her seat, ordered another Ginger Ale, and finished listening to her favorite opera.

Her headphones blocked out the scream that came from the next person to use the bathroom.

To find out more about T. Gamache
and his books, visit
www.indiesunited.net/t-gamache

Fishing Ain't Fishing

by Michael Deeze

When I was a boy, my father would occasionally take me fishing. He was not prone to company at most times, preferring the solitude of self-reflection and the comfort of his own agreeable opinions. To be included in his plans at any time was a celebrated event, but fishing had its own mystique about it. Fishing assured more personal time with him than I might otherwise receive in an entire month. A taciturn man was my father, having no patience for extended conversation—or additional acquaintances. I believe it was his considered opinion that he already had too many as it was.

My father was an incredibly patient man—when it came to his own activities. Often spending many more times reflecting on a chore than on the industry required to accomplish it. Not indolent, rather stubbornly committed to not hurrying himself into poor performance. For a fishing trip, he would lay out his fishing gear, painstakingly examining even the smallest piece, respooling his reels, organizing and reorganizing his lures, and sharpening his hooks. Often taking a week in preparation for a day-and-a-half of weekend fishing. Working in silence, but in plain view, building in me an excitement that rivaled that of the week before Christmas.

Only after his gear had been stowed in the car, and his thermos of coffee had been filled would he seem to recall that other people also existed in his world. He might then ask for accompaniment and then wait impatiently with the engine running for the selected one of us to quickly pack and be ready to go with him. These trips usually began on a Friday night after a long work week, and we would drive into the oncoming darkness and disappear into the mystery of what lay ahead for a young boy.

Fishing for my father, and his father before him approached that of a spiritual experience. Not in a religious sense of the word, but because it offered them escape from the restrictive structure of being a responsible adult. For them it was not just about baiting hooks, or cleaning fish. For them it was something else entirely. It was the state of mind and body that they maintained within while they performed these mundane activities. A task meditation and it was a rare occurrence that the two of them did not experience it together. It was a lesson that I was slow to learn, taking years and mountains of living experience before I understood the depth of it or its meaning.

My grandfather, tall and razor thin, with hands as large as shovels, had labored in the lumber camps of the Northwoods, cutting timber and gandy-dancing the logs down the river in the spring. My father, raised in the lumber camps, also razor thin but smaller in stature with delicate clever hands like his mothers, was the more introspective of the two. They would often spend an entire weekend together without having spoken more than a paragraph of sentences between them. Their understanding of each other and the world around them observed and appreciated in the silence of togetherness.

On the road, driving through the night while I slept in the back seat, I would often awaken chilled and alone. The car parked in front of a wayside tavern or road house; the two men inside; anxious to start their weekend. Eventually returning and continuing on while I rode in dreamy half-sleep.

In the early morning light, with the sun clearing the horizon and the mist thick on the surface of the water, we would emerge and stretch. We found ourselves in a world of pine scented forest, and a racket of bird calls. A world ruled by nature and where men were scarce. While the two men carried their small rowboat to the water, I would unload the car, stacking the gear at the water's edge. Once the little boat had been floated and the oars were in their oarlocks, they would pack the gear carefully. There was fishing tackle, bait buckets, and stringers for the fish that might be caught. The bulk of the space in the boat however was taken up by a case of beer, a cooler for sandwiches, whiskey, and ice. In the event that a large musky or pike was caught, or a large snapping turtle sighted, there was also a .22 caliber rifle and my father's WWII service automatic. There was no need to pack ammunition, the guns were never unloaded. Although it is never possible to 'hurry up and relax', my father and grandfather knew a few shortcuts.

What little space that was left in the boat was for me. I would take my place, jammed between the beer case, cooler and spare tackle into the curved bow of the boat, sitting directly on the hull, my life preserver stuffed under my butt. An experience that while satisfactory at that time of the morning, lost its appeal as soon as the heat of the midday sun made its effects more noticeable.

Grandfather sat in the middle, within easy reach of the oars, facing backward. My father seated in the stern facing forward, face-to-face with his father. As Grandfather's great shoulders and hands took the oars and with strong strokes would propel us rapidly away from the shoreline, rowing until we reached a seemingly arbitrary location on the river or lake. Once there the two men would drop the anchor and begin readying their baited hooks. You could not ask the fish to hurry to the bait, wanting them to destroyed the point of fishing in the first place. Both knew it took a long time to fish for five minutes, and both knew how to wait.

Instead, they set their baited hooks attached to bobbers, and let the bait do their work for them. As soon as this was accomplished, they would toast each other with a swallow of whiskey and open the first beer of the morning. For them, sitting in the boat a beer in their hand, watching an osprey search the water below for its breakfast was the existential point of the trip. My job, crammed in the bow, was to watch the bobbers as they slowly drifted away from the boat, alerting the two men of any possible bite.

After the day had warmed, and a few more shots of whiskey had taken their effect, the two would attempt to educate me as to the point of the lesson. My father would speak of the boundary that existed between the two worlds, that of the rarified atmosphere above the water's surface and the dense alien world that existed below. The world that I could feel vibrating through the quarter inch of aluminum that made up the keel. He would speak of the wonder of living things that could no more survive in our world than we could in theirs. He would tell of the multitude of variety that went about their lives unknown by us, existing only a few meters away from us but separated by millions of years in evolution. My Grandfather, would speak of the alien world above us. The birds and insects that inhabited it, and we, grounded in our earthly forms could not. Somehow, these two men who rarely spoke in multiple word sentences, communicated the state of joy these creatures inhabited—unhurried and unworried.

They would point out the trees that lined the shore, alive and ever patient, uniformly bent by years of enduring the steady north winds. They would point out the shifting sandbars, changing shape and location in the river, alive in their own way, constantly in motion, smoothing the river stones over millennia. Through it all they smoked their cigarettes, drank and pointed, nodding to each other, sharing their silent speech and understanding and saving their words for me.

Although I appreciated the sights and sounds around me, and listened attentively to them I watched the bobbers more intently. The anticipation of catching a fish kept me alert and anxious, looking from one to another, imagining the slightest motion as an impending strike. The day would pass, and the beer case would slowly empty and the cold sandwiches; pulled from the cooler and eaten.

The two men, tired by the all-night drive and an early start of their day, would then pull their hat brims down and doze in their seated positions. I was unwilling, and unable to do the same should I miss a fish. I fantasized the feel of a living thing at the other end of the thin line, the tug and the struggle, and the eventual victory and heroic return home. The need for patience difficult to muster, and hard to maintain.

On one occasion the sunlight dappled the water into millions of sparkling diamonds and I lost sight of the bobbers in the brilliance. Rising onto my knees I peered into the brightness fearful that I would miss the most important event of the day. My father, roused by my sudden activity and sudden rock of the boat, looked up and smiled.

"Son," he said, "if you are fishing and you're doing it right, catching fish should be an interruption."

And so it was.

To find out more about Michael Deeze and his books, visit www.indiesunited.net/michael-deeze

H2LiftShips: Just Passing Through

• ● ⬤ ● •

by Bob Freeman

Introduction

This continues our H2LiftShip saga, visiting the untold communities in the Asteroid Belt.

Our team on the H2LiftShip, the*LunaCola*: Captain Grace, the First Mate, and the rest of the crew made their way through the cosmos, looking for customers and profit.

Approaching the Asteroid

First Mate held the sextant steady in three of his arms and sighted on the North Star, quickly taking a reading as the *LunaCola* picked its way forward in the inky blackness. The sun was aft, and stars and galaxies barely resolvable, just tiny points of light. The ship was alone in the void, with no islands of sentients, ships, or rockets for millions of kilometers in every direction. In their 360° bubble of nothingness, they drove forward, pushed by the solar stream and the boost from Earth's gigantic Lagrangian laser cannons.

First Mate clung to the periscope, hugging it, scanning for their target, floating in the same emptiness of Sol's vast heliosphere. They had speed and now had to slow down to match the orbit of the asteroid spinning and moving in front of them. The Captain turned the three-meter-tall wheel to bring the ship about. She barked a command to the speaker tubes,

"Bring in the spinnaker for the change-over." The two crew members, Jack and Tang, suited up and went out the top airlock to deploy the triangular sail. The First Mate flipped up an arm to signify that the course correction was true as they began a tack to slow the ship down against the constant flow of Sol's photon onslaught.

Each tack, port to starboard and back again, slowed the ship down and brought them closer to the asteroid. As the asteroid traveled along its ordained path, the ship continued the tacking maneuver to slow its forward motion, flying toward the sun for a photon brake.

The asteroid wasn't metallic and shining nor gray and dull as were many of its neighbors in the void. Instead, it sparkled and shimmered in the distance, bright against the darkness. They were still a few days out, and this was the most entertaining thing they had seen for a while. Everyone started naming the colors they saw, trying to be the first to recognize and claim them in a freestyle game. The primates were pretty good. The canine, as expected, dead last. The octopus quickly won this game, naming a few colors in the infra and Ultra-red ranges. It could have been fibbing since no one else could even imagine those colors and the names assigned.

The crew was used to seeing the spinning Crookes radiometers standing out from asteroid edges and the shiny solar cells, giving the illusion of living rock or a shiny hirsute caterpillar.

Captain Grace had already contacted the local political leaders, the Jefes of this rock, and contracted for a laser boost to get them back up to speed after trading was done. Coming to a dead stop was something to be avoided on these solar-powered ships, far from the intense core photon stream.

The rock continued to flash all the Earth-Rainbow colors as they drew closer, but the patterns said nothing they could understand.

Captain Grace sent a Morse code message asking for landing permission, sending the ship's name, advertising logo, and ID for verification. The port officers were expecting the ship, and the merchants were ready to trade for the cargo in its hold.

It was hard to determine if they replied to the query since the background display buried the dots and dashes in its ever-shifting colors. The First Mate could normally dig out that information from the background noise but never reported any signal, apparently transfixed by the asteroid's flashing patterns.

Octopus was glued to the periscope, snuggling up for a closer view than unaided eyes. Colors starting flowing from arms to mantle and around again, apparently mimicking the asteroid or maybe trying to respond to its hidden messages.

Coming closer, the colors were not fixed in space but twisting and changing every moment. The asteroid appeared to dance in the void, flashing all of its features in technicolor hues. Fortunately, the landing port was a delightful gray color, and targeting that spot was easy.

The *LunaCola* began its final approach to the tarmac as the ever-shifting colors held octopus in their sway. The human, easily mesmerized by the flashing, changing colors, was not much better than her First Mate. Captain Grace could work with the colors firing off her optic nerves but had trouble resolving the fine structures. She would need to see straight and clear to place the ship on the landing strip, intact.

Tang was no help, the lights just gave him a headache.

It was time to call out the big guns.

"Jack, check out the landing site and let us know the trajectory we need for a soft landing."

Jack cocked his head and lifted an ear asking his Captain a direct question, in doglish. She answered back, using spoken words, and conceded, "Yes, you can use base-4 math for the calculations."

"Captain, we never got permission to land. Shouldn't we wait? "Tang had learned his lesson in the busted poker game on Caerus and did not want to cross authorities again. He wasn't chicken but a nervous Orangutan with the fortitude of mush. Not surprising, since the intelligentsia, prone to over-thinking, always seems to be the weakest when it comes to action.

"No, they know that we are due and they can see us through all that glitter, I'm sure," The Captain always felt that it was important to bolster her crew, even with a weak lie.

Jack took the sextant and dug out his abacus. He was, after all, a bit old school, and a slide-rule was too hard to use with no thumbs. All of the licensed LiftShip crew had to pass a class on navigation. They did not need that skill often, but when they did, they had to do it right. The bioGel display gave him the heading, spin rate, and the ship's speed. He checked the sextant and began flipping the beads around in a manic pattern. It was either fancy calculations or just for show, but no one complained as long as it worked.

Jack gave his orders, something he seldom got do to, "Tang! Time to reef the sail!"

It sounded good, to Jack, to be in charge. Everyone else just let him have his moment of glory.

The reefed sail was set, reducing the push from the core of this solar magnetic bubble, flying along within its galaxy, bound for nothing and nowhere.

Tang rapped on the airlock to let Jack know he was ready. A spin of the wheel brought the ship around to tack back across the solar wind, slowing its forward motion. Another directional change and the ship dropped into an elliptical orbit, each turn drawing closer to the landing zone. One last tweak and the ship was lined up, slowly meeting the upwelling plate of the landing zone. A slight bang resounded through the bridge as they touched the asteroid, stabilized with the Magno-plates against the ship's hull.

Jack set the sextant down on the First Mate's desk with a distinct clunk, "How it go, Captain?"

He wasn't searching for praise, navigation was in his job description and nothing new, but if someone tossed him a jerky treat, he wouldn't refuse it.

"Excellent job, Jack, maybe we can replace the octopus on our next trip out."

Octopus just turned a sickly green color and flashed red on its arms.

"No, Captain, no want navigate-ey job, it too hard." Jack looked over at Octopus, “and scary.”

Green turned to light blue, red to grey, and Jack avoided a conflict he did not really need.

"No need to worry, it was just a little joke," Grace answered, "you both know what a joke is, right?"

Even after being together for many cycles, inter-species jokes were always iffy, almost as bad as a first-night stand-up routine, every time.

Solar Cells

They could clearly see that the thousands of colored banners were made up of small linked solar cells, turning the surroundings into a molehill, closely approaching Avogadro's number from the looks of it.

The banners had strings of colored rectangles held between fine jeweled arms, spinning in the solar breeze. One side a solar cell, the other dark as the void. These puny Crookes radiometers, a spinning wafer, connected to magnetic bearings, a tiny generator, pulsing electrons on every hit of a photon.

Static solar arrays were much too dull for the locals, they wanted power, color, and entertainment in a single package.

Even the magnetic bearings followed the color formula,

each pair a jewel. Rubies, diamonds, and all the shiny hard pieces of carbon, silica, and metals connecting the cells in their shiny grasp.

Minute amounts of pure elements, layered on the glass, interfaced, becoming colored diodes capturing the wayward photons and transforming them to electrons, flowing down the grid. The sun does not miss them nor care what happens to these bits of energy. Once tossed off, they were free to the universe, until their source, after eons, was compressed into a white dwarf.

The colored cells were certainly not as efficient as pure, stable solar cells tuned to the ideal frequency. Still, this crowd of sentients loved the color and the action and would happily waste photons for art. Their motto was that "electricity is as free as a photon."

On the Ground

Jack was the first one down the gangplank. He was ready to stretch his legs and see what type of jerky they had for him to sample. A quick look around and he gave everyone his take on the surroundings, "This place looks funny. Just like MommyEarth, except no gravity, and more flashy colors."

"Oh, no oceans, rivers or red-trees, but same."

Octopus was not far behind, blending into the background. He strode around in his reverse wet suit, three arms stiffened with internal axostyles to become legs. He had little to say, but his color changes mimicked the joy of being surrounded by unlimited, ever changing colors.

Captain Grace donned her official Captain's bomber jacket and blue jeans, with understated jewelry, as falls to her rank and skill.

Grace took inventory of her crew. They were far in front of her, except for Tang.

"Captain, I'll stay with the ship, this place is a bit intense for me."

He still had a headache and was looking for a cold compress.

"I'm sure this is a great, colorful place, but I much prefer variations of green. Don't get me wrong, I don't mind a few bright fruit colors, but," He trailed off on his excuse. This cacophony of color was a bit much for his sensitive soul, and eyeballs.

Octopus was in heaven, he dove into colorful camouflage as they came across every dynamic banner. It's as if he was made for this world. It was almost like his Earthly ocean with its blue-green mottled moving colors. He tapped out to the Captain,

- ....

.. ...

.-- --- -. -.. . .-. ..-. ..- .-.. --..--

.. ...

- .... . .-. .

.- -.

--- -.-. . .- -. ..--..

"This is wonderful, Is there an ocean?"

"Sorry, this is as dry as the other rocks," was the disappointing answer she had to give.

Jack had his doggles on, and the flashing colors had little effect; his blue merle coat with hints of red and white made him look almost normal in this environment. His hat and cape, purchased in Niland, offset his beautiful fur.

The threesome, or two, if you couldn't see the octopus, walked out to meet the merchant sentients.

A little girl, primate, probably human, ran by the trio and stopped as Grace bent down to say hello, "My Air is your Air, Niña."

"Mommy, how come the colors are so drab. It hurts my eyes!"

"Milaso, please, some travelers only have a few colors, we don't talk to them about it, they can not help it."

"But Mom, look at the solid color, how can they stand to be so monochrome. I would just die!"

Big words for such a little girl, but she made her point.

"Hush child, it is rude to bring it up, you will have to learn to accept all sorts in this universe."

Grace thought, *This wasn't in the travel brochure.* Another attempt at humor, but no one else heard it, fortunately.

Taking the conversation to heart, Grace went back up the gangplank and found her only colorful garment, a tie-dyed shirt she had picked up in that Earth-Retro-Hippie town, as a joke.

Back on the ground, she looked almost normal, blending in with all of the outlandishly dressed citizens of this rock. Only her blue faded jeans gave away the fact that she was not a local, but she would not exchange that fashion statement for any other.

"Well, that was interesting. We're off to a good start," she told no-one in particular, *In the future, I'll research a colony and not trust the Chambers' of Commerce brochures. Don't want to make that type of mistake again!*

She hurried along, catching up with Jack and maybe octopus. It was hard to tell exactly where that camouflaging beast was walking.

Merchants

Each asteroid group seemed to specialize in a particular commodity. Those closest to Sol grew food and used water bubbles for farmed fish. The ones with abundant minerals or ice are miners. Carbonaceous asteroids, with nothing much of value, became centers of government and exchange houses.

This shiny, colored rock did not seem to have anything

much for export, and their solar cell arrays were not as efficient as other plainer cousins.

The merchants and re-sellers, clad in dazzling colors, were waiting by the warehouse entrance. There was no unique emblem or pattern to distinguish the buyers in their patchwork of bright, glaring, almost psychedelic panels.

Captain Grace put her hand on the octopus' wetsuit and tapped out:

.-- .... ---

.. ...

.. -.

-.-. .... .- .-. --. . ..--..

"Who is in charge?"

Octopus, with his excellent reasoning ability and sharp eyes, just gave a shrug color. This was weird even for him.

The leader, clearly recognized by his bright colors, virtually identical to everyone else in its randomness, greeted the team, "Welcome travelers to our little paradise. You honor us with your colorful dress. My Air is Your Air." This may have been an attempt at humor. Except for the octopus, the crew of the *LunaCola* were a bit faded compared to the locals.

After airy greetings and a few unusual looks were exchanged, tea and real Earth water was offered to those who needed a beverage. Formalities complete, everyone well-hydrated and finally, the big question, "Did you bring the goods?"

Jack didn't drink tea and took it upon himself to answer, "We no have druggies, but lots of stinky cow poo. Is that what you want?"

A pause, then "WHY?"

The leader and his assistants seemed to be taken aback by that question and broke off, forming a discussion circle: mumbles and muttering, long looks and narrow eyes.

Jack knew that this was directed at him, *did I say something wrong?* He asked Captain Grace in doglish.

No, that was a good question, replied Captain Grace, using the same language constructs. She was sure that the merchants did not know what they said. Using doglish and the octopuses' color language could give them an edge in any future discussions. Octopus could read doglish, not as well as Morse code, but serviceable. He signaled acknowledgment colors to the Captain.

Grace rolled this information over a bit. *Seems that these colors hide a darker side, the sentients seemed to be particularly picky and sensitive. Oh, well, not much different from my family, and I know how to work with that.*

Chief Jefe broke out of the circle, which then unwound around the trio. It seems that their discussions were over. He told Jack, "herbs are our specialty, we use earth supplies to make up for growth in ZeroG"

The *LunaCola* carried bags of quality earth soil, and a few dozen cubic meters of Earth's finest cow manure, the favorite substrate of *Psilocybe cubensis* and a tasty supplement for many other plants and fungi.

Jack, always the inquisitive canine and treating the discussion like an interesting bone, "Why need stinky stuff, not have cowies here? Me know they make this."

The Jefe, now identified by his extra foppish touch, looked at Jack with extreme disdain. It was almost as if he didn't like dogs. "We require the best, enriched, organic nutrients for our farms and Earth dung is the best. Our plants really seem to like that touch of home, but you probably didn't know that."

Jack, didn't let that bone loose, "Me prefer other parts of cow-ies. You got wrong end." A toothy grin emphasized his point and direction.

Captain Grace stepped in, Jack was right, but she still had to sell her stock of manure. It was doing no good in the *LunaCola's* hold and was a little odorous. It would probably take a long time to vent out that smell. The sooner it was off-loaded, the better.

"We are willing to trade our 36 cubic meters of manure for an equal volume of your finest herbs and teas. We would be satisfied with that exchange." Grace tried this ploy to bring the merchants back to focus, she knew they would not accept it, but it was a starting point.

Jefe looked up, shook his head, sending colors shimmering, "Well, not on a one-to-one basis, but you have had a long trip, please join us at the table for more tea, salt, and some of our local bread."

Grace thought, *good, at least the formalities don't require the Vodka, bread, and salt routines usually offered.* She emphasized her agreement with the offer, "Yes, more tea would be fine."

Grace was ready to go inside away from the shimmering, disconcerting flashing colors. "Jack, I'll need your help on the exchange, this sparkling place has me a little lightheaded."

His tail started, up and down, then around. He did not have much to work with, but he put it to use. He seldom got to participate in the art of the deal, but this time, he was top dog.

The Deal

The merchants placed samples ready for inspection; exquisite leaves, twigs, branches, powders, and fungi. This was their big chance to exchange their products for something they desperately needed, Earth-born dirt and poop. They could always sell to other traders, but all they got in exchange was food, Standards, and hardware. This brown gold in *LunaCola's* hull would keep them growing for quite a while.

Grace asked, "Jack, can you scan those codes and snap a picture of the products?" She did not want anything to do with more colors. Even glancing at those QR codes made her head swim.

Jack's bioGel-powered comm read the standard 4096-color QR code labels and translated the colored lines to readable text. Of course, octopus did not need the help of those gooey tablets, he could read, translate, and even display those codes, all at once.

It was obvious to anyone who had ever been to Earth that the samples were a little stringy and light compared to their full-gravity-grown counterparts, living 1AU from their filtered light source.

A deal point and Captain Grace grabbed it, "These are not up to the same color-depth and quality of the Earth grown samples."

She let that sink in to see what the counterpoint would be.

"Yes, we admit that they are not as intense as Earth grown plants, but what is? We are closer to our customers and the extracts seem to work the same no matter where they are grown."

"We export our diverse colors and brightness to the drab citizens of the belt, it is always in demand."

If the octopus could snort, it would, talking about color to these cephalopodic chameleons was laughable.

"Colorful clothing, jewelry, and herbs, both tasty and enlightening is what we offer, you will find no better this side of HomeWorld."

One of the lesser merchants, a baby Jefe so to speak, broke into the conversation, "and receive the best prices for it."

Jack finished his checking routine and tossed the results to Captain Grace's bioGel, it did not help. *This is all gobblygook, I still can't think straight after the light show.*

"Thanks Jack, let's spend some time reviewing this data."

Maybe looking at the 'gel would clear things up. It was gray and black, to soothe the tired eyes.

The display showed blocks of products, grouped in boxes

with a picture and text. Each box held four samples, but nothing necessarily related to another. Grace tried a few changes. Maybe *there was a pattern, Box 1, first item then box 2, second item? No, that didn't work.*

Octopus, looking at his Captain's obvious distress, reached over with a light tentacle touch and the ‘gel re-configured, everything in a nice, related list. Grace looked up, nodded to octopus, and with a subtle color response, acknowledged acceptance.

Grace spent a while, longer than needed, but the gray display was so refreshing, she did not want to rush the process. The flashy merchants were getting nervous, and that was a good thing.

Grace offered a price for the exchange, they countered, and so it went on. Jack started getting bored as he always did during these interactions and looked around for some jerky treats. He quickly scanned his copy of the list for something interesting, finding 'catnip' but no 'dognip.'

Jack figured *If asteroid need to import manure from Earth, probably not any good jerky around.* Maybe he should protest, but he remembered that he had some fine Earth-beef jerky stashed in his cabin and decided not to make a big deal out of some dry, ugly leaves and sticks.

Captain Grace and the Jefe and his companions stepped back, a deal was sealed, and the exchange was started. Grace's head cleared a bit after smelling those fresh herbs and tea leaves and she made a great deal in exchange for her supplies. This was good news. She could re-supply her tea collection and make a good profit along the way. These plants were hard to find once leaving the environs of HomeWorld, even if their essences were not up to Earth's standards.

No matter what, coffee was still out of reach. No one had ever found a way to grow those beans away from the warm, friendly gravitational hug of HomeWorld. Good thing she had switched to tea during her Academy training.

The ship's dirt and manure were exchanged for locally grown products, not at the 1:1 level Grace had wanted, leaves and twigs were not as dense as cow paddies. The last container, filled with dried mushroom powders in tightly sealed bins were carefully carried up the gangplank and secured.

Tang, a little leery of that last product, brought up his concerns, "Are all of these dried herbs and powders legal?"

Jack agreed, "We not want not-legal cargo."

The Captain, more concerned with successful commerce than complete legality, did not ask those types of questions. "Now boys, I'm sure these fine folks would not sell us anything that was not legal, everywhere." Internally she considered what they might be getting into and decided to take some precautions. She considered, *another reason to double-check the Chamber of Commerce brochure for each colony on the route, better make sure there is a legal market for the products before bringing them out.*

"Tang, please check each bin and bring me the read-out."

Her years of experience acting as a logistics manager, for free, on her family's ship taught Grace that it was prudent to validate cargos before leaving port.

"Let's make sure that the labels match the product. "

She handed him a bioGel probe, one end with an open sniffer, the other with a fine short needle. Tang knew all about bioGels, but Captain Grace still gave him an unneeded bit of advice, "be gentle, the 'gels don't like probe insertions and we don't want to get them angry."

Tang was now in charge of validating the herbs, a job that meshed well with his jungle upbringing. He could have taken a sniff and a nibble, but the chromatography attachment displayed the material's composition in greater detail. The 'gel also reported any unforeseen reactions that could affect a sentient of any species.

"Please wear gloves and don't eat the herbs, we don't know how they will react with your metabolism until we get them characterized." Captain Grace was concerned for both the product and her crew. She really did not want an intoxicated, large, hairy simian off his center. She needed all of the crew awake and on point, always.

Tang meticulously checked the bins, the bioGel uploading the sensor results and analysis to the connected 'gels on the ship. Apparently, none of the items were especially toxic and some would have medicinal value on the more remote settlements. A few had more intoxicating characteristics, and those had value too. Most of the settled asteroids were able to convert yeast and sugars to beer and vodka, carefully curated, identified herbs and mushrooms were nice supplements to the boredom of space and gig work.

Passenger

A primate, human, apparently male, dressed a bit drab compared to the other citizens, came up to the Captain and Tang. Greetings were exchanged, and he stated his purpose. "You have to get me off this rock, I can't stand the pretentious, flashy, drug-induced life here."

Paying passengers were always welcome, Grace let him continue.

"Everyone has to wear those dammed tie-dyed shirts and bandannas. It's worse than the military, so many colors, it is impossible to figure out what your rank is."

A pause, waiting for agreement or acknowledgment. Neither one was forthcoming.

"I hate that head covering, and those swirling, flashing colors...Please!"

Still nothing

"I can pay."

A pause, Tang picked up his ears.

"I have Standards."

Well, that was an ungulate of a different color. A nod from Tang got the Captain's attention. "Where do you want to go, citizen?"

Implied, how much do you have?

Our lost soul touched his comm and displayed a number, "Will this get me off this rock and onto another?"

The number displayed was certainly enough for transport with air, food, and waste handling included. The plea continued, "One that is drab, preferably."

Tang looked at the Captain, she nodded, and he welcomed the new passenger aboard, "My Air is Your Air, my name is Tang. We can take you, we leave in 3 rotations, bring only luggage you can carry."

"Yes, My Air is Your Air, my name is Jonas."

LunaCola had room for more than a few cubic meters of gear, but it was important to set limits to any paying passenger, just to let them know who was in control.

"Mr. Tang, I'm already packed, and will be here and ready before launch."

Laser Boost

It was time to leave this overly intense little rock, Captain Grace, and certainly, Tang would be happy to get back to the calming, inky blankness of free space. Octopus would probably dream about these colors for a long time, and Jack was just concerned with his carefully selected jerky treats.

Captain Grace reminded the Jefe that they had already contracted for a laser boost, "We need a 50-megawatt boost as per our contract."

Jefe looked at his tablet, "I'm afraid that you did not specify the wattage, we can only give you a standard 10mw boost, 2 rings. The other 40mw's are an additional fee."

As with most spinning rocks in this part of space, the boost lasers are in a ring around the center. Each one fires off in sequence to push LiftShips in a straight line. Each laser on this asteroid was 5 megawatts. The whole sequence would be required for a 50mw boost.

Our Captain glanced at the contract she quickly brought up on her ‘gel. *Damm, forgot to ask about the power levels for the Laser boost. Now I'll have to up-charge all of my customers to make up the unexpected expense.*

This is not what Grace had expected. She tried a different, more aggressive approach, "I thought you said you had a laser boost. Your puny little 10mw light will barely get us off this rock."

Jefe, hiding a smile, badly, "Well, we do have a catapult, it is only half the fee of a full laser boost."

The crew and their new passenger heard the discussion. Tang looked at Jack, "Don't worry, our Captain will get this taken care of."

From the look on her face, this may not have been true.

Nothing resolved in the ensuing moments, and finally, the passenger broke in, "I'll pay the fee, just consider it my gift for getting me off this *mishigas* rock.

Grace did not like taking gifts from strangers but might consider an exception to this rule, "Tell you what, we will consider that your transport fee and call it even, My Air is Your Air."

"Agreed, I am honored to be able to help, My Air is Your Air."

No profit would be secured from carrying this passenger, but there was little loss, and he did help them out in a bind. Things could have been worse. They could have lost all their hard work to these less than honest, overly shiny inhabitants.

The ship was trundled off to the laser launch platform, fees paid, spinnaker set and flashes of photons sent them on their way.

Everyone, except maybe Octopus, was happy to see this rock behind them. They had products to sell at other, preferably uncolored, stops.

To find out more about Bob Freeman
and his books, visit
www.indiesunited.net/bob-freeman

Mind Numbing

by T. Gamache

October 31, 2019

I broke my first neck when I was eight back in 2006. I didn't even know I had done it when it happened. I just stared at the stupid PE teacher who was yelling at me and I wanted him to lie down and die. And he did. Just like that. It was the first of many neck breaks. And car crashes and plates broken. But like I said, I wasn't even aware that I had done it. Most of the kids were just scared and screaming as the blood escaped from the corner of Mr. Brightman's mouth. His eyes were wide open staring at my soul like he could see into my messed-up brain like he knew that it was me who caused all of this.

So, I went home after the police came to the school and all of our parents were called to come and pick us up. My mother walked me back to the car and when we got in, she just kinda looked at me with a real worried look in her eyes. You see, my mother is not my birth mother, she is my house mom as I live at a foster home with five other kids. She was very concerned, but I didn't really know why as she had absolutely no connection to Mr. Brightman. She may have known of him, as he was on the town council, but other than that, he was pretty much a complete stranger.

"Are you ok, Mark?" she asked me. That's my name, by the way, Mark Riley. That's not my real last name, but the name I've been given as, from what I've been told, no one knows anything about my birth parents.

"Yeah," I replied. "It was a little scary, but he was mean. So, even though I was scared, I'm not sad. He was a jerk-off."

My mom didn't like that I used that type of language, but she knew that I heard it from the other boys, or quite honestly, the jerk-off that was her husband. He liked to hit us and not feed us dinner if we were too loud while he sat in his chair that smelled like cigar smoke watching shows that had women in very little clothing on.

My mom stayed quiet and was much more concerned than I realized at the time. As years went on, I found myself in other situations where I seemed to be controlling the result. When I was being forced to eat the roast meat that I hated and my mom's husband was yelling at me about it, my plate flew across the room and caught him right above the eye. He needed seventeen stitches and he could never see quite the same out of it. I was never made to eat roast meat again.

Then there was the time in seventh grade when I saw Jonathan Morris flip me off while driving by with his dad. I hated Jonathan so much because he insisted on slapping the back of my head and spitting on me whenever he saw me and also did it to all of the other kids who lived in my house. He said we were the "Lost Boys" because our parents lost us at birth. We weren't even all boys! Freaking jerk-off. So I made the traffic light fail and his dad never saw the semi-truck that was heading at him. It slammed right into the side of his car. The truck's grill had those bull horns attached to it and I watched and smiled as one of the horns pierced through Jonathan's neck. We were never called the "Lost Boys" again.

So as I grew up I used my powers for both good and not-so-good. You might think I just went on killing rampages all the time, but I'm not some crazy psychopath! Settle down, Mr. or Ms. Reader-Person! I just want justice when it's needed. I seemed to not only be able to manipulate inanimate objects to do whatever I commanded them to, but I was also able manipulate my body to learn skills very quickly. So, I learned how to play music. It was the only time that my mind was clear. Completely focused on the music. I learned to play bass guitar and was one of the best for my age.

It was weird because I made these things happen and no one seemed to notice that I was the common denominator on all these grotesque situations. I got good at making things look like random accidents. I continued to manipulate the world around me with no attention until I turned seventeen my senior year of high school. I came home one day after hanging out with some friends of mine as we had just started our punk rock band. We were called The Snots, and we practiced at my drummer's house because his dad was practically deaf and his mom didn't notice as we smuggled beer into his basement.

My mom came into my room, closed my door, and sat on the edge of my bed. This was not normal as we lived in a house with a "no closed door" policy as all the three boys in the house were getting older and she didn't want us in there with the local girls who tended to be sluts in my town. Not that any of us had any luck with chicks to this point, but she wasn't taking any chances. And our two sisters seemed to never be home, not really sure what they were up to, but whatever.

"They know about you." she said. Sarah Riley stood about five foot one and weighed about one hundred and ten pounds soaking wet. But don't piss her off. She has curves that make the men look a little longer than they should, but the mouth that tends to keep them at bay. Women fear her and we loved her, unconditionally.

"Who knows about me?" I asked, feeling a little more than confused at her sudden sense of urgency.

"The government. The feds. The MAN! They know about your powers and that you have been using them. They know you had something to do with the Morris boy's death all those years back and they know it was you that caused that accident at the factory last fall. They know everything."

Let me bring you up to speed. The previous October I made the metal belt on Harold's (that was her husband) machine at his meat packing factory where he worked come off when it reached about seventy-five miles per hour and slice his throat. It was the first time I had killed someone from a distance without having them in my sight. Took a lot out of me and I was sick with flu-like symptoms for three days. Well worth it. Poor bastard. He bled out right there in front of God and everybody. He never touched us again.

"Anyways," she continued, "they've been coming around here asking questions and writing down stuff and generally taking notes. They are going to lock you up if you don't leave with a quickness." I loved the way Sarah talked to me, but right now, I have to admit she was freaking my shit out a little.

So, I came to find out that my mom has always known about my "specialness". She watched me closely from when I was young and just pieced things together. For a while she said she wasn't sure if I was aware that I was doing this or if it was dumb luck. Then she realized with the Jonathan Morris situation that I knew exactly what I was doing. She just let me go and never said anything. Even when I killed her old man. I think she was relived if you ask me. The hitting wasn't only limited to us. She came in with her share of black eyes, too.

The next day at school I found myself keenly aware of stares and looks that I had never noticed before. I found myself feeling nauseous around certain individuals and I wasn't sure why. Until late in the day when my science teacher, Mr. Berube, followed me into the boys bathroom.

"Hey there, Mark. How's your day so far?" he asked. He was opening the janitor's closet that usually contained a mop bucket and some crap they throw on the floor when the freshmen puke up their lunches. Not a normal stop for a science teacher. That was my first clue.

"Fine" I replied. I was having a really weird day and making conversation with this pot-bellied, balding creeper was not my idea of passing the time. Especially while I was trying to take a piss. Please stop talking.

"Do you think you could give me a hand here for a second? I need to move this crate of supplies out of the way to get to the fuse box, but I can't get it by myself." He was not really making eye contact with me as I was walking towards him.

I instantly got really nervous and anxious and this is when my "powers" always start to kick in. I found myself able to sense I was in danger and it was like I could sense the gun he had in his hand. What was he going to do? Kill a student in the bathroom and just leave me here? Maybe make it look like a suicide?

As he turned towards me, I grabbed his arm with my thoughts and jammed the gun right through the 220-volt breaker that was located inside the fuse box. The metal barrel made contact with the electric current and he began to shake violently. His flesh started to burn and blood was coming out of his ears. I threw him across the room and made sure his skull smashed the side of the ceramic sink caving his forehead in. He slumped to the floor as I walked calmly over him.

My mom was right. They were everywhere now, and I had to get out.

So, I left that afternoon with two hundred dollars in my pocket and never looked back. That's the thing with being a foster kid with no record of birth parents. You can pretty much pick up, change your name and never look back. I found a job a few hundred miles away and got myself an apartment. I hooked up with a touring rock band and have been on the road for the last three years. I've never really had to use my stuff that often anymore. Maybe a jerk-off club owner or someone trying to swindle our cash away from us. But nothing more than a broken arm or two. Or maybe a sudden stroke if the asshole was worth it.

And that's how I ended up here. Alone in my hotel room with a girl from the club last night. I have had my share of one-night stands these past twenty years or so, but this one was different. She seemed special, if you know what I mean. She had been flirting with me all night and when we finished our last set, she made sure that I knew where she was going to be spending her evening. Not that I minded at all. We had a great time and we finished off more than enough alcohol to put us both into a hung-over state this morning. She slowly got out of bed with a hair style that has seen better days and gives me a coy smile. We both had the walk of shame look going on.

"I'm gonna take a shower. You can join me if you want." She stripped off my t-shirt she was still wearing and made her way into the bathroom and I heard the shower turn on. Not a bad way to start the morning, right?

I smoked my last cigarette and gave her some time to get the water hot. These hotels can have pretty shitty water pressure, and we're not rock stars, so we usually end up at the closest Comfort Inn. As I walked into the bathroom, she caught a glimpse of me in the mirror.

"It's about time. Take your clothes off and get your ass in here." she said as she had her back to me and was looking over her shoulder.

I opened the door to the shower and heard a thud followed by a gurgling sound as she hit the floor. I saw the twelve-inch dagger that she was planning on using on me sticking out of her chest as I perfectly placed it in her heart, or I should say, I had her perform the kill. I would love to be inside their heads as I take over and command them to do the unthinkable. She wasn't bleeding too bad as I kicked her out of the way and took my shower.

You see, what they don't know is that as my mind has

grown stronger and older, so have my other senses. I can smell them now. The ones who are out there trying to catch me. I'm not sure yet if they are government or some special underground corps of lunatics, but they are out there and they are trying to get closer. Like the guy I ran over with the bus last month. I know that they are everywhere, but they have no idea what I'm capable of. What they also don't know is that my body is becoming as flexible as my mind.

I reached down and touched her shoulder. Slowly she started to shrivel up into an unrecognizable solid mass on the white tile floor. Her hair was the last thing to burn and the smell was a combination of onions and shoe leather. You know one of those smells that you can't decide if it is good or gross? Yeah, like that. While this was happening I could feel the changes take place in my body. I was morphing and shifting and things were changing all over the place. I was getting smaller and my inside were re-arranging themselves. It had been a long time since I had taken the form of a woman. I didn't enjoy it as much as I was not used to the amount of sexual flirtations and forwardness that men show. It usually doesn't take me long to find another unwilling volunteer, usually as the result of said flirtations, and I can put myself into the shape of a male again. The transformations usually last for a month or so while it allows me to skip town. Then magically, one day I am back to my original self. Weird huh? Yeah, you should have been there the first time it happened…

To find out more about T. Gamache
and his books, visit
www.indiesunited.net/t-gamache

Radhakrishna

by Bharat Krishnan

When the sun hit Davana at just the right angle, the native bay-backed shrikes would come out to bathe in the warmth of this hidden village. The white underbellies and small, grey tails of these birds did nothing to distinguish them on their own, but a black bandit mask over their eyes made them universally recognizable as the *Mascots of Davana.* Ubiquitous and yet unique, the portrait of colors was what made them so beautiful.

"Krishna!"

Yashoda called into the neighboring woods for the God of Love to return home after a day of school and then playing with his cousin, Balarama. She heard his bare feet crunching leaves and twigs below before seeing his cherubic face emerge from the trees nearby. It was impossible not to smile. It had been 13 years since his birth, 13 years since his birth father had entrusted her with his well-being. The eighth avatar of Vishnu had been born to Vasudeva and Devaki at that time, but Krishna was not safe with them. The boy-god's uncle was the evil king of Mathura, Kamsa, and he knew of a prophecy that his nephew would one day rise up to slay him. And so, Vasudeva had broken out of jail for one night with the help of the gods themselves to deliver this baby to Yashoda. Kamsa had tried coming for the boy, but after many years of trouble they were now secure enough to wait. To wait until the boy was ready to fulfill his destiny.

"Coming, mother!"

He did not know the truth about himself, not yet. How could a mother place that burden on her son? No, Yashoda would not rob her son of his innocence until it was absolutely necessary.

The boy would leap over the threshold of the house in previous days, his black feet landing with a thud to shake the foundation of the building. Landing on one foot with the other raised to his hips, he'd extend his arms out and strike a pose as Shiva, Lord of the Dance. Today, though, he tiptoed inside as if worried of waking a lion. His face was bowed in deep thought, and the cricket bat he'd brought in from outside dragged mud into the house when he entered.

"What's wrong, *beta*?"

The God of Love did not even acknowledge his mother, simply choosing to sit down at the table and wait for dinner. She'd heard from her friends about the hormones of teenage boys; perhaps not even the gods were freed from them. Setting a stack of thepla down as she sat next to him, the pair ate their multi-grain flatbread in peace. She had prepared his favorite curry of okra and spices, but he ate it all so fast she wondered if he could even taste it.

"Tomorrow you can spend more time outside if you want," she said.

A smile wandered across his face as if it was lost. "Thank you, mother. I'll go to bed now." Cleaning his plate, he retreated to the safety of his bedroom and closed the door. As Yashoda listened at the door, she heard Krishna's sniffles.

Krishna woke the next day before his mother had a chance to pester him. Explaining his pain to her would be like sharing a secret with one of the village's bay-backed shrikes – wrong and pointless and unnatural. The burden and beauty he held in his heart was between no one but himself…and Radha. He'd first seen her yesterday, while playing cricket with Balarama and the others. He'd hit a ball so hard it went soaring into the forest from the schoolyard, and when he chased after to retrieve it he came across her group. They sat on stones and gossiped about boys by the river, and their skin was as fair as the payasam dessert his mother sometimes gave him and his friends as snacks. Krishna dreamed her skin smelled as sweet too, but he didn't dare approach her. Even through leaves and shrubbery, her body shined like Lakshmi's herself.

"Whoa…" Krishna dropped his cricket bat in awe, and the sound was enough to alert the girls to his presence. Mouth agape, he bent down to grab the bat and lost ball before turning around and racing back. He never saw Radha's smile as she batted her eyelids at him. He missed seeing her blue and yellow saree up close as she moved towards his hiding place with the lithe grace of a dancer. Krishna might have pretended to be the Lord of the Dance, but in Radha he had accidentally found the real thing.

All Krishna could think of during school that morning was whether or not he'd get the chance to glance at Radha's face once more. He'd figured out that she was a year above him, which filled his body with relief as he could not bear the thought of sharing a classroom with her. It would've been impossible to mask his longing to brush his hands against the same wooden desk she sat at and smell her hair as she walked past him at the water fountain and smile when she laughed upon hearing a joke. Their separation was agony, but it was what kept him sane as well. What did school matter? He would be fine knowing nothing else as long as he knew her.

"Krishna?"

"Hm?" His math teacher had asked him to come up and write an equation. "Sorry, ma'am." She chided him, but he did not hear that as well.

During lunch, Balarama gathered another group to play cricket.

"We have another half-hour, man. Let's make the most of it."

She would be in the forest again, he knew it. He would hit the ball as hard as only he could when Balarama bowled it at him and it would fly into the forest and then Krishna would have an excuse to go talk to her. He dared believe she might even be impressed at his strength. And so his friends rose and he followed until they found themselves in the field by the school once more. Krishna agreed to bat first, swinging the bat so fast it kicked up dirt from the ground that stained his white pants but matched his skin. The sound was like thunder when bat and ball connected, and again Krishna ran to secure maximum points before going to retrieve the ball. This time he would leave the bat behind lest he disturb the girls like yesterday. The wind whipped against his muscles as he darted to the forest; he'd never been so alive. When he saw Radha once more, her eyes carried a kindness in them he had only read about from fairy godmothers.

"Who's there?"

This time it was Krishna's bare feet that had alerted the girls to his presence. For a moment, he locked eyes with Radha and he knew his mind was not clever enough to pull tricks on him like this. He could not have imagined her mouth breaking into a grin or the whiteness of her teeth or how her neck reflected the sun when she threw her head back in laughter.

"Come play," she said. "Come join us if you are so keen on our company."

As she stepped towards him, he hesitated before looking down at his bare hands and feet; he had never before been so aware of his dark complexion. Turning away from her, he ran.

"Who was that?" Radha asked one of her friends.

"I think that was Yashoda's boy, Krishna..."

Krishna returned home that night as glum as Yashoda had ever seen him, and it was then she'd decided she'd had enough.

"Enough of this moping, *beta*." She rolled her eyes as she doled out a potato and eggplant curry for them to eat with tonight's thepla. "What ails you?"

"You would not understand, *amma*."

"Oh," she nodded in mock thought. "What a puzzle you are. It's a girl, right?"

"*Amma!*" He almost knocked his plate over in shock. Had he not been as cool as he thought?

"Your mother is no fool," Yashoda said as she sat down. "I could even tell you stories about boys in my day."

"Please don't!"

She smiled before taking a bite from her food. "Then tell me about this girl."

"Oh... how could I begin?" His appetite evaporated when he thought of her, for their love provided all the sustenance he'd ever need. "Describing her with words would be like trying to explain math by dancing... besides, nothing will ever happen."

"And why not?"

Looking down at his dark complexion, he gave voice to his fears at last as only a boy who trusts his mother can. "She is as fair as the law of dharma, while I was born as black as a bull."

"My child," Yashoda crooned. She was as flexible as any other mother; strict in one moment, teasing in the next, and soothing thereafter. "Has anyone ever made fun of you for that?"

Krishna stared at the ground so hard Yashoda wondered if he aimed for it to swallow him whole.

"No... but that does not mean she could not be the first."

Staring at his long legs and sharp jawline, his mother sighed. "You are good looking by any conventional standards."

"Mother," Krishna sighed before standing up, his plate of food untouched. "Even the term good looking is a subjective word imposed by the masses to enforce antiquated ideals about what is beautiful and what isn't. What does conventional matter? The only opinion to value is Radha's."

"You are good at sports and decent enough in school," Yashoda said. "Any girl would think you're a catch."

He paced like a caged lion across the kitchen, yearning to break free and yet worried of strength he had never tested. "Radha is not just any girl."

"No other boys in town have a sensitivity to complement their muscles and brains," Yashoda pleaded. It was not good for her son to deny himself food. More than anything she wanted to end this matter by telling him of his celestial lineage, but it was not time yet. "With brains, brawn, and sensitivity, you are truly the complete package."

"A package she still might ship away," he lamented.

Pulling at her black hair, Yashoda grit her teeth and steamed in frustration as if she was a dragon. Her nostrils flared to a point that Krishna actually sat back down and tore a piece of thepla to eat. "*Amma*... it's good."

Returning to her calm self, she asked him again. "Why do you think she'll reject you?"

"*Amma*, my skin is as dark as the moon. Radha deserves the best."

Leaving the kitchen for a moment, she retreated to her bedroom to grab a few packets of something.

"Here," she said, holding out baggies of powdered color. "Radha deserves the best, right?"

"Yes, *amma*." Taking the baggies in his hand, he marveled at the blue and yellow and pink and green. "But I do not understand the meaning of this."

"Who are you to say what is best for her?" His mother was smiling again, with her eyes and mouth and soul. "Give her these packets and tell her to paint you whatever color she desires."

Again Krishna's friends wanted to play cricket the next day and again he agreed. Only this time, he held the colored packets from Yashoda in his pant pockets. When he chased his ball out today, he called to Radha and she excused herself from her own group to meet him at the edge of the forest, where a boy's formal education and thirst for the wilderness of love intersected.

"I'm glad you've talked to me today." She spoke first; she had much to teach him in the way of confidence and intelligence. Her lithe body sparkled when she moved, each step reflecting the sun off the blue and yellow saree she wore. She was all the colors of the rainbow, so of course his mother had been correct. Of course she deserved whatever colors she wanted.

"I was afraid you would not like my dark skin, so my mother suggested I give you this for you to decide what color I should be." He handed her the baggies, and she received them as a gift. Ignoring the giggling of her friends behind her, she opened the pink packet and scooped some powder out on her fingers.

"I have accepted your gift, and so now will you accept mine?"

"I will accept anything you give me for the rest of time, so long as we can be together." She giggled now as well before smearing strands of pink across his forehead. Then Balarama and the other boys came to see why their friend hadn't returned yet, appearing just as Radha switched to green to smear across Krishna's cheeks. And when Radha's companions joined them, they looked on and marveled as Radha turned Krishna's nose yellow and brushed his chest with hues of blue.

"It does not matter what color you are born," she said. "It does not matter because it is our differences that make up the beauty of this world."

Then the two danced in front of their friends, uninhibited and fulfilled, and Radha withdrew a flute from her saree so that Krishna could serenade them all. The pair were seen together so often that they became known as Radhakrishna from that day forth, and their love and respect for each other grew as intense and blinding as the sun. And once each year, the pair would lead the rest of the town in a celebration of their love that became known as Holi. They would throw powdered color at each other to mark themselves in all shades and hues, for it was that portrait of colors that made them so beautiful.

To find out more about Bharat Krishnan
and his books, visit
www.indiesunited.net/bharat-krishnan

Random Acts of Kindness

by Lisa Orban

A random act of kindness can sometimes happen when least expected and most needed. It is not always the big things in life that can restore faith in the world, but often the small acts that affect us most.

In 2006, during the first part of, my then husband, Billy's deployment to Iraq I could have been the poster child for going postal. My secret longing was to steal all the yellow "support our troop" magnets off of vehicles and then find someone with a "we support Bush" bumper sticker and plaster their car with them. During his deployment I had often experienced indifference and apathy from many people. While the vocal support for our troops is often heard, there is very little in the way of genuine help or support for the families of these soldiers. It was a very long and difficult time for my family and myself, but a small random act during Billy's leave changed the way I felt, and it gave me hope for the rest of the time he was away.

Billy's leave was coming to an end; he was scheduled to return to duty on July 4th. We decided the night before he left to take all our children out to dinner, to spend this last evening with him together before he had to leave us once more. We took everyone to a local buffet, when you have seven children in tow, buffet is always a good idea. As we went through the line I noticed a sign that said this was their 4th of July buffet, when I reached the front of the line I jokingly asked if they had a military discount. The cashier responded, yes they did, Billy handed her his military ID card and left with the children to find us a table, and I stayed behind to pay the bill. While writing out the check I chatted with the cashier, telling her that he was going back to Iraq in the morning and we had decided to take our children out for one last meal together as a family. I thought no more of it as I handed her the check and returned to my family.

Shortly after returning to my family our waitress stopped at the head of the table holding a piece of paper in her hand and announced that it was our lucky day. While talking to the cashier earlier someone had overheard our conversation and after I had left came forward and asked to pay our bill. The piece of paper in her hand was the check I had written and she handed it back to me with a smile. Billy and I were both stunned and we asked who had done this so we could thank them for their generosity. The waitress explained that the person who paid it had requested it be done anonymously; it was a thank you, to Billy and our entire family and for the service we have all given to our country, there was no need for us to thank this person in return.

It was the kindest act of generosity that anyone has ever shown us, and it touched the both of us deeply. Never before had anyone unknown to us ever done anything so compassionate. They asked for nothing in return, not even our thanks. By that simple act of kindness they had restored my faith in the world, and I no longer felt so alone. It's the small, unexpected acts of kindness that touches most deeply, and it brings tears to my eyes even now when I think about it, that someone cared. It means more than any bumper sticker or any mouthed but empty words.

Our family would have liked to have said thank you to

whoever did this for us, but we can't, but I can let others know of their kindness. For every random act of kindness a single person can make a huge difference in someone else's life, bringing just a little more joy into what can at times seem like a cold and lonely place. Because of this person's actions I was able to endure Billy's deployment just a little better than before, I no longer felt as alone or isolated because I knew somewhere out there, there was someone who had taken the time to say, we know and we care.

To find out more about Lisa Orban
and her books, visit
www.indiesunited.net/lisa-orban

Sins of the Father

by Michael Deeze

The top story in the news tonight at six.

> *The search continues for the person or persons that took the life of Susan Jenkins, the eight-year-old whose body was discovered in an alley on the near north side this morning. Police are asking anyone that might have information to call the local 'TIP' hotline. Details of the murder are being withheld while the police continue their investigation. Stay tuned for further updates as they develop at six as the story unfolds."*

I switched the television off and stood at the window looking out at the setting sun. I hated this feeling. I hated that I had no choice. I hated that action was necessary and that I was compelled to supply it. Most of all I hated that I was one of them, one of the scum, perhaps not anymore, but once I had been one of them, the takers of souls.

Now I was a worse thing. I did not indulge in the self-righteous thinking of right or wrong, but I knew a heinous act when I saw it. I knew that there was no need to balance the scale, both in justice and atonement. I knew that I had a lot to apologize for but I didn't need any of that to justify what needed to be done.

§§§

He betrayed her trust and took her innocence. His penis a weapon, his instrument of destruction. There will be no first dates, no first kiss, no high school prom dresses. There will be no second-grade. He took her life.

Her death, only the first. Her mother and her father will follow. Doomed to still walk the earth, still with breath in their lungs, but a heart that will never heal. Their grief a contagious thing, will spread to others.

The police are searching for him. I knew where to look. I knew where he was. When he thought we were kindred and had bragged to me.

The red mist rose in my veins. The beast awoke.

The police will not find him. He is in the ground. I sent him to hell.

I will join him there someday. As the darkness within grows stronger the beast will take me there.

The darkness knows my name.

§§§

Leaning back in the old rocking chair, my big boots resting on the porch railing, provided a frame for me to look through as I gazed out over the front yard toward the road in the distance. Dust hung in the still air marking the passage of a car long minutes ago. The open window behind me brought the sound of my wife and boys cleaning up our dinner dishes as they talked and laughed through the operation. I sipped the last of my iced tea and felt the contented fatigue that comes after a long physical day.

The evening sunlight slanted in under the ancient oak trees of our front yard making long shadows that stretched all the way into the barnyard. It was too early for the dew to start to fall, but the heat of the day had ebbed toward coolness. The weather had been so dry for the last two weeks that I doubted there would be much dew when the time came. Today had been a hot and dusty day.

The hay we had brought in today had been short as the heat of July had given way to dry weather in August. We had only managed just over six-hundred bales today and the hayloft was going to need another crop in late September if it was going to be enough to get us through the winter. With the cooler evenings of late August, the milk production had picked up a little and the bigger milk check would be welcome when it came next week.

Sipping my ice tea I heard before I saw the sound of a truck laboring up over the hill as it approached. I watched as it hove into view and slowed in front of the house. I knew the truck and knew that it was going to turn into the lane. Its appearance and eventual arrival marked an emotional downturn to the pleasantness of the evening. Barely slowing, the truck turned into our lane throwing loose gravel into the ditch and grass at the entrance as the rear end slewed around on bald tires. Billowing dust followed as it clattered its way down the long graveled drive toward the house.

The truck and the driver were a familiar sight in the neighborhood. The truck had been on its last legs for as long as I'd known the driver. The driver was Harland Kincaid. Harland was easily the laziest man I'd ever known. What Harley lacked in work ethic he emphasized with poor hygiene and an almost complete disregard for polite social habits. Harley put food on his table by finding clever ways to take advantage of other people. He was an expert at extorting, cheating, and lying to get his way and his arrival in my driveway meant that he'd chosen his next target. By his appearance, you might think that he was an ignorant yokel of low-intelligence. You made that judgment at your own peril, Harland Kincaid was not a nice man, he was sly and clever, and as far as I knew—without scruples.

The dogs, who had been sprawled on the porch next to me taking their ease after the heat of the day, recognized the truck by its sound, and almost before it had come into sight they were up and standing at the front steps. When the truck had slewed into the driveway they leaped to the grass, surrounding the vehicle before it was halfway to the house, barking with their hackles raised and teeth bared. The dogs, you see, were excellent judges of character.

Once the truck stopped near the front gate, Harley turned it off while the dust of the driveway caught up with the truck and the engine coughed itself to a fender rattling stop. The dogs stationed themselves on the driver's side, but far enough away to avoid tobacco spit, while Harley hurled insults in their direction. He was definitely smart enough not to venture out of the truck without permission.

To say that I didn't like Harley would have been an understatement. My father had told me that Harland Kincaid was the biggest waste of breath in Monroe County, and had never had time for him. He had once taken me to Harley's house on an errand when I was younger and it had been a singularly memorable moment in my young life.

The house was ramshackle, tarps nailed over holes in the roof and waist-high grass and weeds in the yard hid all manner of broken rusting farm equipment, tree stumps and featured a dead dog lying next to the front steps. When my father asked him about the dog, Harley had said that he shot the dog because he got sick of feeding him. Now he smelled so bad he'd stopped using the front door. Burying the dog or disposing of it in any other way had never occurred to him, he had simply started using the back door instead.

I levered myself up out of my rocking chair and walked out to the gate. Close enough to talk, far enough to avoid the odor.

"Evening Harley."

Harley finished yelling obscenities at my dogs and turned his head one-hundred eighty degrees. He couldn't turn anything else because his big belly was trapped behind the steering wheel of the old truck.

"Yeah, it is. Still hot too. And dry." He scratched a spot somewhere under his armpit and squinted toward the barn. "Got all of your hay in?"

"Workin' on it."

"I'm gonna be needin' to get some before the snow flies."

"It doesn't put itself in the barn you know."

"Mine does. Say you ain't heard nothin' about me lately have ya'?"

"Like what?"

"Oh nothin', just wonderin' if anybody's been asking about me lately." He decided to try the door handle of the truck, and both dogs were immediately on their feet. He just slammed the door and tried to twist toward me again.

"Like what Harley?"

"Oh nothin', probably shoulda' stopped over at your dad's and asked him, but you know, he's not home much these days, and it's away out at the other end of the ridge."

"He's not home much any day, house calls and working at the clinic. He does have a job you know."

"Yeah, yeah, should be thinkin' about retiring. I would be", he took as deep a breath as the steering wheel would allow and let go with a long greasy spittle of tobacco which cleared most of the passenger window, but not all, "he's been kinda cranky lately."

"Cranky? With you? Hard to believe, what'd he say?"

"You know, same old shit, I charge them Amish too much to drive them to town." He said Amish, with a long 'A'. "I told him it was none of his business, cuz' it ain't."

"He does it for free all the time."

"His loss, twenty bucks is twenty bucks. Besides some of

them is kinda cute."

"Pretty sure they're not lookin' for a date, Harley."

"Harley's always lookin' for a date," He smiled and actually mustered a wink at me, "especially them one-night kinda dates."

"Well then, you're probably shoppin' in the wrong grocery store there Harley."

"Just the same, them young'uns don't have much fun, I bet they're just dyin' to play a little 'slap and tickle'." This time his gap-toothed smile leaked tobacco juice down the front of his shirt and he actually giggled.

I took a deep breath and looked out past the barn while I counted to twenty. My father had taught me that the reason some people were put on this earth was only so they could serve as a bad example for the rest of us. If that was the case then Harley Kincaid was at the top of his game. Harley had a way of making people want to punch him in the mouth. He couldn't afford to lose any more front teeth though and I was more inclined to just turn the dogs on him anyway.

Out on the road, another and much quieter truck crested over the hill and slowed at the lane, before turning in. My father's truck looked just as tired and dusty as I was beginning to feel talking to Harley. Harley looked in his rear-view mirror and started.

"Oh shit, that's your dad. Well, I guess I took enough of your time Sean, good ta' see ya, say 'Hi' to the missus."

He started the truck on the second try and was already rolling before my father made it all the way down the lane. Making a wide circle in the barnyard, Harley rode the ditch beside the lane past Dad's truck and out into the road, before motoring away in a cloud of dust and gray oily smoke. Dad rolled to a stop and shut off the truck. This time the dogs wagged and whined anxiously for the driver to step out for a proper greeting.

Instead, the passenger side window rolled down and he spoke from the seat.

"What did that worthless piece-of-shit need today?"

Opening the yard gate, I walked over and leaned on the passenger-side window sill.

"No idea Dad. Dinner's just finished wanna come in for a beer?"

"Can't, there's trouble down toward Hustler."

Hustler was a little wide spot in the road at the far eastern end of the ridge. There was a gas station, two taverns, the Amish cheese factory—and a stop sign.

"What kind of trouble."

"Amish girl, Rachel Hochstetler's missing, apparently since early this morning. She left for school this morning but didn't get there. Someone else taught the classes and so she wasn't missed until chore time tonight when she didn't come home. That's when they found out she'd been gone all day. The sheriff's called out the Civil Defense guys, so I guess I'll go down and see if I can help out."

"Rachel one of Jonas' girls?"

"Yeah, I guess. I talked to the sheriff, she's thirteen. She's just started teaching lessons at that schoolhouse down at the bottom of the ridge off of County 'A'."

"Well, shit. I'll go too."

Sometimes you get a feeling that you just can't shake. And sometimes that feeling comes with a certainty that you know is absolutely true. I took a moment and looked up the lane where the dust still hung in the air from Harley's truck.

"I might need to stop off on the way through so I'll drive my truck too. Give me a minute."

"You done with your chores already?"

"I think I might just have one more right now."

"You need some help with it?"

"No, but thanks Dad, I gotta get something from the house.

You go on ahead, I'll catch up. I gotta run an errand."

My father looked at me, then his eyes widened. Twisting in his seat, he looked back over his shoulder.

"You don't think? Well shit. That son-of-a-bitch.!"

§§§§§

In the house, I got my hat and knife off the top shelf and ran my belt through the loop, and put it in my back pocket. Nice and secure, like Dad taught me. Turning for the door, my wife blocked the exit.

"What's going on Seth?"

Thirty seconds was all she needed for the light to come on in her eyes. But she still had enough common sense to see where I was taking it.

"You are not your Daddy, Seth."

"No, I'm not Nora. Not by half. He's not that man anymore either. He left it behind a while ago. But I got a bad feeling about this and just right now, I might be mad enough to be more Dad than Seth."

"Why don't you just call the sheriff?"

I thought about the dead dog laying in the front yard at Harley's.

"Because if I'm right and the sheriff pays him a visit, I can't imagine what might happen to that little girl before they stop him. I think we'll just go have a little talk.'

"Is that your Dad's kind of 'little talk' or yours?"

"I guess we'll see, sorta depends on Harley."

§§§

Thirty minutes later I was sitting on the road at Harley Kincaid's mailbox. The long dusky evening had given way to full dark. The western horizon still bright as the cloudless sky slowly surrendered to a quiet summer night. The tree frogs and crickets were in full throat. The mailbox next to my truck was the only sign that there was a habitation nearby. Harley's driveway was nothing more than two dirt tracks straddling high grass disappearing into the trees. Unless you knew where it was, you would drive past it without a second thought.

Leaving the truck behind, I decided to walk the hundred yards to the homestead hidden back in the woods of the little valley. The noise of the night creatures was so loud that I didn't really need to be careful about making noise, but I minded my steps just the same.

Coming around the bend in the lane, the silhouette of the house and outbuildings was outlined against the remaining light from the sunset. Near the fallen down shed that used to be a garage, Harley's old truck 'ticked' itself cool as I passed it. From the front, no lights appeared in any of the windows, and the appearance of abandonment was complete. The cool night air was fresh with the smell of grass and the surrounding woods, but the slight breeze carried the smell of hot grease and fried meat.

Leaving the worn path between the truck and the front door, I skirted at an angle between the old barn and the house, wading through waist-high grass as small creatures hidden there rustled and scurried away. In spite of the dry weather, within seconds my pants were soaked with the evenings' dew, and my socks dampened inside my boots. As I moved along the side of the house there were no lights visible inside of the house, but a small one appeared to my right in the barn.

I detoured toward the barn and approached the old milk house at the near end. A broken pane in the little four-pane window in the side of the room showed where the light escaped in an otherwise filthy opaque glass, and a single incandescent bulb lit the room dimly. I eased up to the window and chanced a peek in through the broken pane. Old milking equipment, milkers, hoses, and buckets hung on various nails along the wall and the monstrous stainless-steel bulk tank took up most of the floor space in the room. In a wooden chair directly opposite the window sat a small absolutely still girl with her hands folded in her lap. She still wore her black travel bonnet and shawl and she stared straight ahead seemingly lost in thought. There was no sign of Harland Kincaid.

I waited another few minutes to see if Harley was nearby, or not around. Almost immediately music blared across from the house as someone turned on a radio tuned to a country music station.

Good enough for me. I skirted along the side of the building to the door. A metal hasp secured the door from the outside with an unlocked padlock hanging in the loop. Pulling it out I tossed it in the grass and pushed open the door. Rachel Hochstetler looked up, her eyes wide with fear and surprise. I raised one finger over my lips, signaling her to remain quiet. Crossing to her I kept a safe distance but squatted down in front of her so that we were at eye level.

"Hi Rachel, I'm Seth Casey. I think we should get you home now. Is that all right?"

"You are the doctor's son." Not a question. Her voice was a little shaky but she was showing remarkable control and her gaze was steady.

"Yes, Dr. Casey is my father."

"I would like to go home."

"Are you alright, did he do anything to you?"

"He locked me here. I have been here this whole day."

"Alright, that's good." I looked back over my shoulder and thought for a moment. "Okay, I'm going to go talk to Mr. Kincaid, I want you to walk back down the lane. My truck is at the end, by the mailbox. Go ahead and get in the truck, and wait for me. I'll be right along."

She didn't speak but nodded. After checking the door

again, I sent her on her way, a black silhouette disappearing into the darkness, and turned toward the house. I didn't know where the path to the house was so I tried to strike a straight line through the tangle of tall weeds and thistle. Almost immediately I tripped over some hidden piece of broken machinery and fell face down.

"Who's there?! Who's out there!?"

Untangling my feet and getting back up on my feet in the darkness proved to be tougher than it should have been, and it took me more than a few struggling moments.

"What are you up to, Harley?"

"Goddammit, I've got a shotgun here, who's out there?"

"What kind a' game are you playin' Harley, what's going on here?"

"Is that Seth Casey? What the hell are you doin' runnin' around in my back yard?"

"I come to get the girl Harley."

"Ain't no girl here."

"Not anymore there isn't."

"What! What the goddamn hell! Listen you smart-assed son-of-a-bitch you get off this property right this goddamn minute or I swear to god I'll open fire!"

"My dad should be bringin' the sheriff around pretty quick Harley. Think it might be a good idea to have a little talk, maybe before things get out of hand."

"We ain't doing no such a thing, you get outta' here. I'm sick of you Caseys. Always too good for everybody else, always got two cents for every sich-iation. I'm giving you to the count of ten Casey, then you get a load of Double-B's in the ass."

I had been moving toward the back porch as we talked. Not hurrying, but making progress. The light from the kitchen gave a little light and made my progress a little easier. When I stood at the bottom of the steps I looked up at Harley.

"I think this time you might just have put your foot in it,

Harley. You gonna rape that girl, or just have her over for dinner?"

"Mind your own goddamn business Seth, this ain't no affair of yours. Sides them 'A'-mish don't tell no tales. You can do what-ever, and they just forgive ya. I'll just get me a little forgiveness when I'm done."

"Well, I hope you've got plenty of Vaseline, Harley, cuz the girl is gone."

"What! You let her go? Where at? Where'd you put her? You son-of-a-bitch! I'm gonna blow a foot-wide hole in you!"

It took two quick steps to hit him with my shoulder and propel the two of us through the kitchen door and across the floor. The pump shotgun clattered away across the floor as we both scrambled for traction among the debris of the littered kitchen. Harley outweighed me by a good hundred pounds, but it was all uneducated flesh and he huffed and puffed his way to his feet slowly.

"Gonna kill you, Casey."

"So you say, Harley. Shall we give it a try?"

§§§

Mornings are always my favorite. The smell of the barn filled with cows and the 'chug' of the milking machines. The calves, bleating for milk, and the cats roaming the center aisle in search of any milk spills. Cold mornings the barn is warm and hot mornings the barn is cool. It is the most contented I ever am when I'm doing the morning milking, choring with my wife, and feeling the magnificent independence of putting my own food on my own table.

Today was no exception. That is until I turned toward the milk house with a full pail of milk and was confronted by two scowling faces, standing in the center of the aisle. One scowl was one I was completely familiar with, having elicited it since I could walk. The other was no less significant, but I'd had less experience with it. Behind them, my wife stood with a bucket in one hand and an 'O' where her mouth used to be.

My father came right to the point.

"Sheriff needs a word… and for that matter so do I."

"You got me at a bad time Dad, but we're almost done. Can it wait a bit?"

"This isn't going to wait, Seth," Tom Hawkins had succeeded the last sheriff, Jim Peters, and been re-elected for almost twenty years. He was slow to judgment and quick to action, and exceptionally popular. His was the other scowling face."

"Well, let's get away from the compressor then. Honey, I'll be just a minute, would you change machines when they're ready?"

We stepped out into the cow yard at the end of the aisle into the bright sunshine of the new day.

"What's up, Tom"

It was my father that spoke.

"Last night you said you had an errand to run, right after you had a conversation with Harley Kincaid. Then Rachel Hochstetler turns up back at home, with nothing to say about where she was, or who she was with. This morning Harley is laid out on the slab in the coroner's office with a fractured skull as the preliminary cause of death. What's your explanation Seth?"

"Rachel's home? That is great news!"

"Seth, you seem to maybe have information about Mr. Kincaid, or at least you had a discussion with him. You may be the last person he spoke with"

"How did it happen? What happened to Harley?"

"His place is one of the most disgusting places I ever seen. He was lying at the bottom of the back porch steps face down, and appears to have struck his head. There was so much crap scattered everywhere it would be impossible to determine if there was a struggle but there was a cocked and loaded twelve-gauge shotgun on the floor in the kitchen. His right arm was broken as well."

"He fell and hit his head? Wow! Can't say that I'm shocked, but that's a tough way to go. Just sayin'"

"Just sayin'? Honest to god Seth, that's all you can add?" My father's eyebrows were in danger of disappearing under the brim of his hat. Tom Hawkins was looking me dead in the eye.

"I don't know anything about what happened to Rachel or Harley. I went over to Norwalk and looked at a bull that I want to borrow for next season. After that, I went straight to Hustler. When I got there the search party had dispersed, so I came on home. You can ask Nora."

My father put his hands in his pockets and looked out into the pasture ground.

"Well, I guess that's that, Tom."

"I guess. But I'll need to get a statement from you later, Seth."

"Okay by me, let me know."

Tom turned and re-entered the barn, heading back to his squad car while writing in a small notebook. Dad turned back to me and sighed.

"Shame about Harley. I always felt pretty bad about that damn dog of his." He looked back at the barn watching Nora change milk pails. Beyond that the sheriff's patrol car passed by the door on its way out of the lane.

"I'm too old for this shit, but that's not a road I'd ever want you to go down, Seth.

He turned to go, and made it halfway to the barn before he turned back, "but I'm glad you handled it just the same."

To find out more about Michael Deeze
and his books, visit
www.indiesunited.net/michael-deeze

Starting Over

by Leslie A. Piggott

August 1, 2012-Lucy

Every day for the past three years, I have sat on this bench at 5:30 a.m. waiting for the city bus to pick me up and take me to work. And almost every one of those days for the past three years, the same woman has jogged past me. She always smiles, waves, and says, "Good morning." She seems to actually enjoy the fact that she's sweating before six in the morning.

Of course, I wave back and smile. I imagine that she considers me to be one of her fans, cheering her on as she gets her run in for the day. She probably even has a name for me: Bus stop #44 lady. She is probably one of those people that always has something positive to post on Facebook or Twitter. "Ran 10 miles today. Feels amazing." "Date night with the hubs. #blessed" "Best kids ever." Because, of course, she has kids… of course she's married to the next Captain America. I haven't decided yet if I think she's a professional or a PTA mom. I mean, I know, it's been three years, but it's not like I'm stalking her. I just watch her.

I know what you're thinking. I am not "Girl on the Train." Obviously, I'm riding a bus here, people.

August 3, 2012-Paige

Every morning since a few months after I lost my job, I've gone for a run. I run past some of the same things every day, partly because they are right by my house and partly because I like to have some familiarity, though not *too* much. You never know if there are any crazies out there stalking you or trying to stalk you. It is kind of fun to see familiar faces along my route too. Like the girl at the bus stop. She's there pretty much every day. She always waves when I wave now, though I doubt she hears me say, "Good morning" as I pass. She always has her headphones in. I still say hi though. It's good to be friendly. That's what my husband says anyway.

"Stay positive, be friendly, people like friendly." I am positive, darn it! Positive that I've failed. He doesn't understand though. He hasn't failed or experienced failure firsthand. He knows only success. He doesn't have the faintest idea what it's like to be anxious or afraid. He has only confidence.

August 4, 2012-Lucy

I have started trying to get here early, just so I don't miss her. When she doesn't run past me, I try to imagine why. Did she oversleep? No, she seems like the type that wakes up before her alarm and is excited to go running. Is she sick? No, she is probably one of those people that still runs even when she is sick. Are her kids sick? Is she out of town? She probably takes amazing vacations. Part of me wants to take up jogging again so I could run alongside her, see where she goes. I won't do it, of course.

I wonder if she notices when I am gone. I'm only gone when I'm sick, or pretending to be sick just to have a day off. Maybe she has an imaginary life pegged out for me too. Probably not. I'm vanilla. I'm nobody.

She is obvious a dedicated runner. I've noticed that she is often wearing shirts from races that she must have participated in. She probably plans her amazing vacations around her races. Then the social media post can include the amazing view along with the amazing accomplishment. "Grand Canyon today. 10k tomorrow." She does marathons too. I've kept track of her shirts... I think she's run about 12. This makes me think that she's the PTA mom, not the executive mom. Who else has time to train for that many marathons? It's incredible how much information you can glean from fifteen seconds of observation.

I tell myself that this could be my life too. My life had the potential for being amazing. Sometimes I think my life is the result of making the wrong choice in one of those "Choose Your Own Adventure" books. You remember those, right? Where you have to choose to follow the mysterious dog into the forest or floating down the river on a raft only to discover that the river ends in a treacherous waterfall and... well, you remember. The choices seemed innocuous at first, but inevitably one of them ended much worse than the other, though I'm pretty sure there were several ways to get the worst ending option. I always got the worst ending option. It seems only fitting that I'd have a life that no one envies.

August 6, 2012-Paige

I think about the girl, well, I should say woman, she's obviously an adult. I'm just pretty sure that she is younger than me. Anyway, I think about her a lot while I'm running. She's the only one I see with any regularity. There aren't a lot of people up and at 'em at 5:30 a.m. She probably thinks I'm crazy for running like this. Maybe I am. I always said that I wanted to be a runner, well now I have the time to do it. I only run this early because he gets up for work at the same time. We used to carpool to work and I'm used to the time. Our budget is tighter now that I don't have a job, so I had to get all my running gear, well not the shoes, you can never skimp on shoes, at Goodwill. I feel a little duplicitous wearing all these marathon finisher shirts. I'd like to run a marathon one day. Maybe that would give me some confidence.

August 11, 2012-Lucy

I was a good student. I even got a college scholarship. I had good friends. I had great potential. I went to college. I didn't even skip my classes. Okay, I didn't skip my classes very often. Everything was going as it should until the unthinkable happened. My brother got into a horrible car accident. Drunk driver. I still remember the phone call from my dad. "There's been an accident." That part of the conversation is clear in my mind. Then it jumbles: "Fatalities... drunk... hospital... totaled." At first, I thought it was my brother who'd been injured, who'd been *the victim.* But no, he was the perpetrator. He was the one who ruined other people's lives that day. He was the one everyone would try not to hate, try not to judge, try not to condemn. I was the one who no one remembered, no one thought about, no one considered.

No one, that is, except the scholarship committee. They were supposed to be impartial, but my scholarship wasn't completely based on my grades. I received it because I'd been such a model citizen, such a good example for those coming after me. I guess when you brother gets convicted of involuntary manslaughter, 2 counts, your community service and charitable acts get overlooked. Lots of people said that it was unfair, that I should fight the board to get the money back. I just wanted to hide and never tell anyone my last name again.

I had a boyfriend back then. I thought it was serious. I'd met his parents. He'd met my parents. We'd thrown around the "m" word. We had one year of school left. The future was bright. Then the future didn't happen, well, not like I had planned. "You choose your own adventure," they'd said at the orientation for college. "You make your own way." Yeah, all that's true until your brother takes it away in one terrible decision. I was no longer marriage material. Clearly, my family was not capable of making decent people.

August 11, 2012-Paige

Thinking about the bus stop woman is easier than thinking about where my life went wrong. They said I had potential. That I was going to go places. I foolishly believed them. That was before, when I was young. When the world was my oyster and I didn't think about all that could go wrong. When I had my innocence.

I sometimes wonder what the bus stop woman thinks of me. exercise-obsessed freaks? I know she's married. I checked her finger and saw the ring. I wonder if she is happy. I can't tell, she never shows much emotion, though who does at 5:30? I wonder if I have fooled her, or anyone else for that matter with my cheerful face and active-looking lifestyle.

August 15, 2012-Lucy

At first, I thought I'd get a job, save some money, and finish school on my own. My parents couldn't afford to pay for my last year, so I had to get a leave of absence. They said that if I came back by the next fall, I wouldn't have to reapply or take any new achievement tests. But, getting a job in a town where everyone hates your family proved insurmountable. Besides, I couldn't imagine returning to classes. Everyone knew. I could see it in their eyes, in their body language. I could finish school somewhere else. All was not lost.

Moving in with your grandparents when you are 21 years old is probably not the tack that anyone hopes to take as an adult. But when your parents get divorced because they can't stop fighting about whose fault it is that their son turned out to be a total loser, you do what you gotta do. Plus, I couldn't take any more of the pity looks that everyone around town was ready to dole out at a moment's notice. They felt bad for the collateral damage, but not so bad to give me a job. Yet another reason why you shouldn't go to college in your hometown. No one forgets. You'll always be the sister of the person that got drunk and killed people with his car.

Don't get me wrong. I know that I sound selfish. Poor me, my brother ruined my life. I am mortified by what happened. Two people were taken from their family without any warning. Two other people now live in a world that no longer includes their close loved ones, their spouse and their child... their dad and their sister. Every year on the anniversary of that day, I think about writing them a letter. A letter apologizing for my brother. But every year I have no words. What do you say to someone who has lost almost everything that mattered to them? I don't know either. Plus, I'm afraid that they hate me so much that my letter will just make it worse. Or someone will find out where I went and this undesirable life I've created will have to move somewhere else. Again.

August 16, 2012-Paige

I took up running because it was something I could control. It was something that I could improve about myself. It had some predictability, which was comforting considering all the unpredictable parts of life. So many people have these lives that seem so simple: go to college, graduate, get a job, get married, have kids. That's what you do in America. 2.2 kids and all that. I was on track for that. I graduated, *with honors* even, I got a job, fell in love, got married, and had a miscarriage. And another miscarriage. Two more miscarriages later, my anxiety had hit the roof. Whenever the two little lines showed up on the tests, I would gather my hope only to have it dashed time after time. I am a failure as a woman.

August 20, 2012-Lucy

Something they never tell you, or maybe it's something young people never listen to, is that once you start a job and start making money, your desire to continue making money is very high. Sure, I had a dead-end job as a checker at Wal-Mart, but I had money. I could save enough to get an apartment and *then* go back to school. There was always more time for school later. I only had a year left.

Every fall, I tell myself that I'm going to find a school that I can transfer my credits to and apply to enroll. I have even gotten so far as to print out an application from one school. It has a lot of compatibility with my old school. It's part of the same system, just in a different city. Going back to school means giving up my apartment. I can't finish school in a year and pay for the apartment. I'd have to move back in with my grandparents. I would feel like a failure again, or maybe I've never given up that feeling.

August 22, 2012-Paige

I hid the anxiety pretty well at first. It's something I've dealt with my entire life. Anxiety is hard to explain to someone who doesn't have it. It can be paralyzing, which is apparently not a good quality for an employee of a cutting-edge Fortune 500 company. I had some paranoia that I was causing the losses either by sitting too much or not sitting enough or being exposed to some teratogen on a phone or a file… the fear of loss was so great that I couldn't do anything. I was afraid that my marriage would end because I was such a failure. My mom often suggested that I see a therapist, talk through my troubles. I think I scared the therapist. She suggested running and cut back on our visits once I started doing seemed so much better. Maybe I am better.

I didn't tell my mom about the babies at first. I didn't want to hear about what Dr. Google told her had caused it or what foods I should eat to make myself more fertile or whatever. Eventually, her nonstop not-so-subtle hints about having grandchildren became too much, though in hindsight, I might have not shouted my troubles at her if I'd just told her to begin with. I was afraid to look like a failure. My husband has taken it all in stride. I'm still afraid that he'll give up on me sometimes, but he still loves me, I think he might even be proud that I've been running so much. It feels good to have someone be proud of you after being a failure for so long.

August 23, 2012-Lucy

The first month, living at my grandparents was great. My grandma made cookies and did my laundry. I was living the dream. They didn't even charge me rent. I think they thought I was going to go right back to school…with student loans or something. They asked me each day if I'd applied to the branch of the college in their town yet. It gets depressing to disappoint people every day, so after 3 months, I moved out. I'd saved enough and had a good enough paycheck to get an apartment. I know I could save more if I wasn't paying rent, or utilities, or everything else.

I don't have any friends. I don't even try to make friends. Friends want to know about who you are and what you do and where you came from. I don't want anyone to know that about me every again.

When I first started watching the running woman, I thought I'd try to steal some of her motivation. She clearly had some to spare. I could take a night class and still get my shifts in. Or I could start running again. Get some confidence that way. Have some success where I used to have success. "I used to love running too, right?" I'd tell myself. Maybe we could be running friends. That could work. Because running friends only talk about running. Or I could make up a story of who I was. But what if she saw me at Wal-Mart? Then she'd know I was really just a loser. Besides, my 6:00 a.m. shift wouldn't work with her schedule. Who am I kidding? She probably barely notices me anyway.

August 25, 2012-Paige

I sometimes wonder where the bus stop woman rides the bus. I'm guessing it's to a job somewhere downtown, though she seems pretty young...maybe she is in graduate school downtown and she does always have on jeans. She has her whole life ahead of her. She'll graduate with her master's or even her doctorate and start teaching at the university or maybe she'll get a part time job so they can start their family. The options are endless... so much potential. She is still young enough to have hope that her dreams can happen. She hasn't seen her hopes dashed like I have. She is carefree, with her headphones and her cell phone. Those days are gone for me.

August 31, 2012-Lucy

Some of the other checkers at Wal-Mart have tried to get to know me. But everyone eventually gets the hint when you turn them down for after work meet ups enough times. Some of them think it's because I'm a newlywed. I wear a fake ring to keep from getting hit on while riding the bus or by creepy customers.

Starting over in this new place was exhausting. This is another of my excuses for not starting school again. I just need to get settled. Find my rhythm. I don't have the energy to re-create myself yet. At first, my mom used to encourage me to see a therapist. Ha! Like I could afford a therapist. I got a self-help book instead. I'm sure I'm just a few more positive thoughts away from getting my life back on track. But, when one of your children is about to go on trial for manslaughter or murder, worrying about your other child kind of stops or just gets put on the back burner until later. Much later, apparently.

About a year after I started riding this bus, I started creating this dream life for the running lady. She has an amazing life, complete with fantastic kids and an incredible husband. She made all the right choices in life and her family is proud of her. Her friends are proud to be her friend, proud to say, "I go to church with her." No one thinks that about me.

In the world I've made for the running lady, all my dreams have come true. The college degree, the doting husband, two perfect kids—a boy and a girl, of course—all of it. She volunteers in her community, donates to the food pantry, and goes on all her kids' field trips. She only buys organic produce and meat and never feeds her kids macaroni and cheese. I'll admit it, even *I* am proud of her. Thinking about all she has makes me want to try harder. I want to have that dream life. They said at college that we could do anything. Maybe part of me still believes that.

September 2, 2012-Paige

Last week, I started looking up races that I could run. Turns out, there are lots of local races here, especially 5k races. My husband saw what I was doing and said that he thought that was a good idea. I smiled at him, but inwardly judged him for patronizing me. I signed up for one anyway. It's in a couple months. I'm a little nervous that I'll be too anxious to do it. I know that sounds crazy. Baby steps. I can work up to this.

I know that I can do the race. It's a shorter distance than I run every day, but there are so many things to worry about. What if I forget to have my favorite socks clean? Or get lost on the course and run further? Or get lost and don't actually finish? Maybe I should find someone to run with me. Not my husband though. I'm sure I'd slow him down and disappoint him. He never says that he's disappointed in me, but why wouldn't he be?

September 3, 2012-Lucy

Tonight, I'm going to go for a jog after work. I'm not going to eat a snack on the bus, I actually splurged on some running shoes, well, as much as you can call it splurging when you buy them at Wal-Mart, and go for a run. I'll get back in shape. I'll ask for a later shift. And then, I'll introduce myself to the running lady, see if she wants to run with me. Maybe I shouldn't though… maybe she likes her time alone. But I could really use a friend, I haven't had a friend in so long. I thought being isolated would be healing. Maybe it was for a time, but I need a connection of some sort. I need someone to be hopeful with me. Hopeful for me. Maybe she needs a friend too. I mean everyone can always use another friend, right? It's going to take a lot of courage to say hi and ask if I can join her for a run. I hope that I don't slow her down. That would probably be frustrating for her.

September 9, 2012-Paige

The bus stop lady has seemed different the last few mornings, almost eager or hopeful. She seems quicker to wave, like she might actually be looking forward to seeing me each morning. I wonder if she knows that I secretly look forward to seeing her too. I wonder if we could be friends if we actually knew each other. Probably not. I'd probably depress her. Though it would be nice to have a friend. I wonder if she is a runner too, she seems like she is in pretty good shape, like she exercises in some way. Sometimes I think I could use a friend. Someone who could listen or just be present. They say exercising gives you endorphins, that endorphins make you happy. Maybe you get more endorphins when you exercise with a friend. I don't know why I'm imagining us as friends. She probably has no desire to know my name. I mean, how would we get together? She is obviously on her way to her job or school when I pass each day. Like she would give that up for a total stranger.

September 15, 2012-Lucy

Jogging is gradually getting easier. I'm able to run a minute longer each night than I was the previous night. I wonder how far she runs each day. Maybe I wouldn't have to go the full distance right from the start. Maybe I could just do a couple miles, tell her I'm getting back into it. What if she thinks I'm lame? Is that a risk I'm willing to take? It's been so long since I've had something to look forward to...something to work towards. Besides saving for college, obviously, I mean, I'm definitely still doing that. I think. I'm just forming a new support network first. A network that doesn't know about my past, or my inability to put it behind me. This could be the first step in good choices for me, not that bad choices got me here. Maybe my loss of motivation was a bad choice. *You can be the change you want to see.*

I put in for a shift change last week. I heard back yesterday that they approved it. It will be an adjustment, but I'll still be up at the same time each morning. I'll just be running first, working second. Tomorrow morning is the day. I'm going to do it. I'm going to show up at that bench, ready to run, and take a risk to make a friend.

September 16, 2012-Paige

Well, the unthinkable has happened. Well, maybe it isn't unthinkable because I *was* thinking it. The bus stop lady, I mean, Lucy, wasn't sitting on the benches this morning. She was standing by it. In running clothes. And we ran. Together.

To find out more about Leslie Piggott
and her books, visit
www.indiesunited.net/leslie-piggott

The Obstacle

by Bharat Krishnan

When I woke up, all I could see was darkness. Overwhelming. The cold water constricted my body like a python. Not content to be merely omnipresent, the snake was growing inside of me as well. While the water crushed the life out of me from without, this creature was tearing my body up from within. I opened my mouth and felt water being forced down my lungs. My eyes stung when I tried to open them, and the darkness around me became hazy. I couldn't breathe. I couldn't scream. I couldn't see. Give up? Was this how I died? NO! I had a mission to fulfill, a destiny.

I have a family waiting for me back home. One moment I was driving to work on I-66, the next moment there was an accident. It was raining; closing my eyes to try and ignore the reality of water surging through my ears to make me deaf on top of everything else, I remembered having to swerve my Lexus off the road to avoid hitting a Semi. My car flipped over the guardrail, landing vertically. I thought I'd wake up in a hospital, but instead, here I am. Fighting for my life. But then again, I'd be fighting for that no matter where I woke up.

How did I get here? It does not matter. I closed my eyes, and let the darkness in. It was unavoidable; nothing I did could cast it away. Best to embrace it temporarily, then. Find its weakness. The things inside us, the people and objects and ideas held by us – those are the ones we can kill. You can't defeat something you can't understand. Come here, serpent. Let me pet you. Let me kiss you. Let me feel your scales and know your face. Then, when you've convinced yourself I'm your friend, I'm going to cut your head off. I'm going to hoist it above my head like Kali, and then I'm going to throw it into the abyss.

The Bikram yoga lessons my husband had insisted on taking me to finally came in handy. Forcing my body to slow itself down, I began to regulate my breath. My lungs were already half full, and I was blind and immobilized as the snake used its watery home to tighten its grasp on me. When everything is out of your control, find the one thing left that you can order and bend it to your will. Focus on that dot, no matter how small, and walk towards it as if it is the light at the end of a tunnel. The light that will guide you home.

For the first time since I woke up, I didn't think about the fact that I couldn't see anything around me. I had four other senses aside from sight, and it was time to use them. Though my arms were weighed down, I focused instead on the seconds of air in my lungs before I'd have to find a way to take another breath. My legs still weren't constricted, and so I heard the cobra slither right in front of me and did the one thing it wasn't expecting – I kicked my legs downwards so that my body submerged itself more fully in the cold water. I fought the urge to scream as my body seemed to cut itself brushing against the icy water, and soon there was indeed blood to whet the beast's appetite. Don't focus on the pain, focus on the goal. As I continued to push my legs down, I repeated the mantra in my head again and again and again and again and again even though the entire journey could not have taken more than two seconds. Finally, my feet touched the ground. I opened my eyes to show the cobra I was not afraid and saw bright yellow eyes staring at me. The serpent was cocky, so sure of itself, so convinced of its invincibility. Being omnipresent wasn't the same as being omnipotent though. Soon, it would know the difference. More seconds passed; I was lingering too long below the surface. Using the very last strength in my body, I kicked as if my life depended on it because it did, and found myself soaring over the snake.

"GOAAAAAHH!"

A breath of fresh air! No time to rejoice; the serpent would be upon me within seconds. Opening my eyes, I saw the room I had been trapped in was actually quite large. And in the center of the room – an Olympic-sized swimming pool. As luck would have it, I had emerged right next to the metal stairs one used to pull themselves out of a pool like this and willed myself to safety just as the cobra brushed against my foot. I shuddered as I lay on the side of the pool, staring right into its yellow eyes as it brought its head above water. The snake had a hood that it displayed now, opening its mouth to reveal fangs that I suppose were meant to intimidate me. I had survived, though, and so what could it do?

As the creature drew itself upright, I realized that the threat had not yet passed. It was so tall, now, that most of its body was above the water.

"HISSSSSSS!"

As the serpent lashed itself side to side, I rolled away from where it brought its body crashing down on the side of the pool where I lay seconds ago. The concrete surface was fractured, yet the animal was not even bleeding. How to stop it?

That's when I saw the weaponry on the other side of the beast's chamber.

It is written in legend that the firstborn of Shiva and Parvati became the God of War, Kartikeya. With a spear as sharp as Kali's teeth and a shield with a rooster on it, the God of War slew the demon Taraka. Honesty. Luck. Fidelity. These were the attributes ascribed to Kartikeya and his rooster shield. All who worshipped him, all who had the good fortune to live among roosters, would reap the rewards of being godly. The son of Shiva was a byproduct of the Ganges itself, and all who spoke his name would know the true meaning of what it was to be lucky and faithful

As must happen to all beings, though, death was not inevitable. Even the gods must pay for their gifts, and so Kartikeya had to return his spear and shield to their home – the Ganges river from which they were forged. And there they lay, for centuries. Until a worthy one could retrieve them…

I had read the texts growing up, the Tolkāppiyam and the Kumarasambhava. I would recognize the spear and shield of Kartikeya anywhere. Hovering above the pool, above even the large snake's hooded head, the weaponry was encapsulated within a blue bubble. This was all so strange, but sometimes strangeness must be embraced. I had a family to get back to, and a duty to fulfill. Dharma beckoned me away from the darkness.

When the serpent picked its tail up and thrashed it at my head, I was prepared. Still controlling my breathing, I launched my body to the left. My arm hit a concrete wall hard, but better that than to meet the creature's wrath. I feared that I would have to pick between the lesser of pains for the rest of my life, but at least I could still choose. The most powerful ability of all was the chance to manipulate one's own destiny.

"RHHEEER!"

The beast was angry that I had not drowned, angry that it could no longer toy with me. Baring its fangs once more, the animal slithered towards me and I let it clamp down on my flesh. There was no way I could get near the weaponry otherwise. I just wasn't tall enough. I needed to lull it into a sense of security, to submit to it in the interim in order to secure a permanent victory. Tears fell from my face as unrecognizable pain surged through my entire body. I would have collapsed right then and there if I had not forced my mind to focus on what lay for me beyond the pool, the snake, and current reality. The mind can take you wherever you need to go, and so at that moment I was teleported back home and saw my loved ones. As the creature's fangs dug into my shoulder, I poked it in the eyes and grabbed onto its neck for dear life.

"RHHEEEEEER!"

It thrashed about the entire room, and still, I refused to let go. Pulling its fangs deeper into my shoulder, I smiled at it through my pain.

"You think wounding me will kill me? It only gives me your strength in addition to my own, demon!"

When the serpent launched itself far, far above the pool, trying to replicate what I had done myself to get out of the pool, I found another spurt of energy to remove my body from its fangs. Throwing myself towards the shield and spear that hovered at eye level now, I slid my unwounded arm straight through the leather clasp of the shield and threw my injured arm right into the spear so that it would always be connected with my blood. The fall to the ground should have killed me, but now I had a God protecting me.

I landed on my knees, and when I looked up I saw the snake was scared for the first time. When I escaped the pool, it was hesitant. Curious. And when it found that I had wanted it to pierce my skin, it was angry. But now, it was scared. Good – let it know what it was like to be the scared one. The beast reared its ugly face at me again.

"RHEEEER!"

"Come at me, Kaliya!"

This was it – the only chance. Fate had spent an entire lifetime sending not only me but also the snake to this moment.

SWOOSH!

"RHEEEEEER!"

On Kaliya's first strike, the spear embedded itself in the creature's hood so that the cobra had to shed what made it seem strong. Now, it looked quite weak as it was reduced to having to bite off the damaged skin in order to save itself.

"RHEEEEER!"

Its second charge was much slower than the first one, leaving me ample time to draw my shield with my good arm. It slammed its full weight against me, and I flew back so that the shield was separated from me.

"It's never easy," I said to no one but myself.

"RHEEER!"

Licking the air around it, the serpent smelled my fear and rose once more to strike. But as it did, I threw myself towards the shield and wrapped my bloody fingers around it as the snake's fangs ripped at my left leg. Its poison was too much. My eyes grew hazy as the beast picked my body up as if it was a plaything, a rag doll to humiliate and enjoy.

"…no…"

As the creature threw my body up above the pool, I remembered what my father had once told me – we must be brave. At all times, we must be brave no matter what. When my body hit the water below, the impact would kill me if the poison didn't first. Still, I would be brave.

My fingers tightened around the leather clasp, and I swung it with the last ounce of strength inside of me. It left my fingers to connect with the giant snake, and when I released the weapon it seemed to pick up speed at an unnatural pace. The shield of Kartikeya spun wildly and did not stop even after it had lodged itself deep inside the snake's neck. The shield of

Kartikeya lobbed Kaliya's head right off, and the animal did not even have time to utter a final taunt before death. Instantly, the water below turned clear blue, and I could feel the warmth of the sun radiate from it even though I could see no sun. When my body landed, submerging itself in the pool, my wounds healed instantly and my strength returned.

"No," a deep voice said. "Not returned…your strength never left you at all."

I was in Kartikeya's home, the Ganges, and had earned his respect.

"Now it is time for you to go to your own home."

Ω Ω

"The end," I told my child after closing the book. Before leaving his room, I turned off the light. After all, darkness was always only temporary.

To find out more about Bharat Krishnan
and his books, visit
www.indiesunited.net/bharat-krishnan

The Plum

by Aaron S Gallagher

1

A glossy black stretch limousine glided to a full stop in front of the embassy. The driver shut off the engine and got out of the vehicle, settled his hat firmly on his head, and sedately rounded the front of the car and went to the passenger door.

He opened the door and handed out a woman. Her legs were bare and shapely. Her red dress was snug but not overly so. She wore matching heels, and retrieved a small clutch from the seat, holding it in silk gloves the same color as her dress. Stepping up onto the walk, she waited while the other passenger, an older man in an expensive suit, stepped out. She smiled up at the Eagle, wings spread over the front of the building. Floodlights highlighted the majestic ferocity of the bird.

She took a small mirror from her clutch and checked her hair, shaped in a beautiful coif of red. She checked her lipstick and eyes. She put away the compact and looked to her escort. He straightened his tie while the driver closed the car door.

The woman waited patiently until her gentleman had fixed his tie. He offered her an arm and they proceeded to the door. Two doormen in white opened the door before them, and they stepped gracefully over the threshold and into the main foyer. The gentleman handed their invitations to the Marine guard at the security checkpoint. He walked them through the metal detector, wanded them both when it went off and patted down the gentleman. After handing over her purse, the wand passed over the woman's body without a sound. A cursory search of the purse revealed nothing but her makeup mirror. The Marine guard saluted, and they proceeded down the ornate hall to the main room.

At the top of the grand staircase, they paused to take in the crowd. A beaming smile on his face, the silver-haired man leaned to his date's ear and whispered something, she laughed gaily, with a voice like a bell. Guests near them looked up at her laugh and admired the couple. She was beautiful, and he was handsome.

The crier at the stairs called in a dignified, carrying voice, "The United States Ambassador to Britain and guest."

Smiling, sleek, and confident, the Ambassador slowly descended the stairs into the milieu, while his date beamed at the crowd.

At the foot of the stairs, the Prime Minister met them. The Ambassador shook hands with him and introduced his companion.

The Prime Minister smiled at her and bent to kiss the back of her hand. She dimpled and said in a sultry voice, "It's a pleasure to meet you, Mister Prime Minister."

"Likewise, I'm sure."

They stood for a long moment, and then the Ambassador turned to her.

"Would you excuse us for a moment, please?"

She looked vacantly between them for a long moment, and then caught her breath as she caught on. "Oh! Oh, of course, Mr. Ambassador." She smiled again. "Mister Prime Minister."

He nodded at her. She headed for the bar and the quartet of musicians playing excellently executed Handel. She could hear the men speaking as she moved out of earshot.

"Tell me now, David, what exactly are you people up to

in…"

She accepted a glass of champagne and sipped while listening to the music. Her eyes flitted from person to person as she took in the resplendent uniforms and dresses, the worldly costumes and mannerisms.

On a balcony overlooking the main hall, she caught sight of the current heir to the British throne and his new wife, flanked by many guards trying hard to be unobtrusive. She smiled to herself.

She kept the Ambassador in the corner of her eye. She was far enough away that she could not overhear him hashing out the details of the current Middle Eastern debacle, but close enough that she could reach him in only a moment.

She smiled at the supposed arm candy of visiting dignitaries. She noted the lack of wedding rings on all of their fingers. They might be window dressing, or they might not. She knew better than most that appearances could be misleading.

She accepted a canapé from a tray and nibbled at the caviar, immediately regretting it. Every time she had an opportunity she tried it, and every time she came away wishing she'd stuck with the flavorless paper it came wrapped in. No matter how expensive it was, or how much of a delicacy it supposedly was, it still tasted like fish jelly to her.

The Ambassador finished his impromptu meeting with the Prime Minister and joined her. She fed him the rest of her canapé, inwardly wincing as he made a show of enjoying the tidbit.

The quartet finished with Handel and struck up some lively Bach. The ambassador extended his arm to her, and she accepted with a smile.

For a few moments, they spun about in the widening dance area, gracefully moving in time to the cellos and viola. As the dance ended, he pulled her into his arms and whispered in her ear again. Again she gave that bell-like laugh and tossed her hair. The close-cut shag of red hair flared like a blossoming flower and settled back again, perfectly in place. Several men watched them with wry smiles, for they knew the Ambassador and had met his wife, and she wasn't this attractive woman. None of the women watching her felt anything like jealousy, for they were with their respective dates most of whom they were not married to.

The woman extended her hand with immaculately shaped nails the color of jade into his silvered, dignified hair, cupping the back of his head and drawing him down into an embrace. Her ruby lips touched the rim of his ear in what looked like an intimate kiss and a promise of future delights. It wasn't.

"So far, nothing," she whispered.

The Ambassador laughed, and said to her, "I'd say you were something," while eyeing two dignitaries on the other side of the buffet table, each responsible for more deaths in their home countries in a year than were born in some developing nations.

"Be serious, please. This is a sensitive assignment."

"I'm aware," the Ambassador said, pulling her into his arms, hands on the small of her back, but only just.

She gritted her teeth and smiled widely.

She watched over his shoulder as more guests were coming in. They had arrived fashionably late, which meant ten minutes after the invitation, apparently. She hated being late and would have preferred to be there first, to get a full roster of guests in her mind before the party became too raucous and boozy to keep track of.

Most people would think that a semi-formal meet-and-greet at the Embassy would be a somber affair, as she had, but it turned out that when you put a bunch of uncomfortable people in a room with slow music and an unlimited supply of good booze, it rapidly turned into a senior prom. She knew that not an hour would pass before dignitaries and their dates would be wandering off into the halls and the gardens to neck like teenagers or more.

Suddenly, the Ambassador was nuzzling her neck, nibbling gently under her ear.

Without changing expression, she pressed down on a nerve under his left arm with her fingertip, making him jump. His arm tingled as though asleep, and he made a startled noise.

"Let's not get carried away, Ambassador. This is business, after all." Her voice was carefully neutral, and she tried not to be menacing.

The Ambassador flexed his hand, rubbing lower on her back while he did it.

"I know, I know. Relax, Cathy." He chuckled in her ear.

She couldn't help herself. She caught his earlobe in her teeth sharply, making him yelp again.

"I told you, Mister Ambassador. My name is Catherine."

2

The party wore on. She had volunteered for this, sure, but didn't like it all that much. She viewed ambassadors and diplomats with the same distrust she viewed beggars on the street; they'd say anything to get what they want or steal it while smiling at you.

She didn't care even for her own ambassador, although at least they spoke the same language, metaphorically. They were from the same world, even if they had taken different routes out. She had dedicated herself to standing between her people and violence, and he tried to accomplish the same thing with words. Like it or not, even Catherine had to admit their track records were comparable.

Ambassador Oren's request for an experienced, trusted agent for a sensitive mission was not unusual. The call had come from her superiors to her because of the ongoing cooperation between her homeland and the U.S. And since the information the Ambassador was attempting to secure was of concern to both parties, she had been summoned from the field to London. Her operation in New York City, tracing revenue streams through the labyrinthine banking system of Wall Street, would have to wait. She would have refused had it not been Commander Halevy asking.

She had been of two minds, wanting to keep up her pursuit. However, the key to the cooperation of the United States, where half of the world's terrorist funding could be traced through fifth- and seventh-layer shell companies and false fronts and drug dealers, was cooperation in kind. She could hardly say no.

In fact, word in the ranks was that she'd have to be crazy to turn it down. An easy assignment in London, a light bit of spy-spy, and a formal dinner party at the Embassy? Who could say no?

She could have, but didn't. She had never turned down a mission, either because of danger or from distaste. That wasn't who she was. Politics didn't interest her, only results. The people she trusted, like Commander Halevy, had goals. It was her job to help them attain those goals. Beyond that, she meant to serve her country. Let others worry about politics. She was a patriot and a warrior.

And yet here she was, resplendent in a gown that would have cost three months of her salary if the Ambassador hadn't had it charged to his personal account at Harrods along with her heels, bag, and the undergarments she thought ridiculous, yet strangely attractive. The wig she wore, covering her natural hair color, and the distracting makeup, designed to change her features subtly but unmistakably, were bothersome but tolerable. She was posing as a secretary from the Ambassador's office, with documents to back it up.

Plum assignment my aching back, she thought diffidently as she stoically submitted to the Ambassador's pawing in his heavy-handed attempt at cover.

She stiffened, incidentally drawing his hands from her behind.

"Ambassador, I think your target has just arrived."

The Ambassador turned her slowly until he could see the stairs from around her neck.

The diplomat in question was squat and heavy, with dark glasses and a huge black beard covering the front of his formal coat. A green-gold sash crossed his expansive middle. Behind and to the left of him was a pale, slender man in a cheap, ill-fitting rented tuxedo. His sandy hair was tousled and he was rushing to keep up with his charge.

"That's him," the Ambassador breathed in her ear. Catherine's skin crawled.

"Be a dear and refill my glass, would you?" Catherine dumped her champagne onto the lush carpet behind him. She held up the empty glass. She extricated herself from his embrace. He reluctantly accepted her glass and turned to the bar. She pulled the makeup mirror from her purse and checked her makeup again, reflecting the scene behind her and unobtrusively watching the diplomat push his way through the crowds, pausing only to exchange words in a brusque tone with representatives known to be sympathetic to his causes. All others he rudely ignored or stared at with unveiled disgust. The put-upon aid behind him struggled to keep up, taking dictation in a battered notebook while trying to maintain pace.

She closed the clasp and dropped the compact into her purse, turning to listen to the band, who were tuning. In the process of turning, she bumped into the squat diplomat, brushing up against him with both hands.

"Oh, my! I'm terribly-"

He pushed her off his suit coat with rough, square hands, muttering under his breath. She lurched, twisted a heel expertly, and tumbled into the arms of the aid, who dropped his pad to catch her.

"Oh!" She simpered and smiled into his harried face. "Thank you, sir! I don't know what happened… so clumsy of me…"

He lifted her gently to her feet, and let go of her arms.

"It-it's all right," he said in a quiet voice, high and sweet. She thought he couldn't be more than twenty or twenty-one. She leaned up and kissed him on one cheek.

"Thank you very much. Very kind. So clumsy!"

"N-no, not at a-a-all," he murmured, with a marked stutter.

She looked into his eyes and batted her lashes.

"Very nice to meet a gentleman. Unlike some others," she said with a quick glance at the squat, swarthy man who had stopped, suddenly aware that he had lost his aide.

She held the young man's gaze for a long moment, then dropped her eyes coquettishly, smiling shyly.

He didn't seem to know what to do with her. He was sweating profusely, nervous and tense. In fact, he was a distant nephew of the diplomat and regarded as quite useless by the angry diplomat, who announced this fact to everyone who would listen.

"I-I'm sorry… miss. I n-need to-"

"Oh, no, I quite understand," she said, with a rueful smile. "A shame, really, but I suppose one has duties…"

"Er… yes." He seemed at a loss.

Catherine looked down and spotted his pad and pencil. She slid gracefully to one knee and retrieved it, automatically scanning the page, her eyes closing once, quickly, like a camera shutter. She flash-memorized the marks on the page. She would be able to reproduce the shapes for analysis later, though she didn't know the language.

She stood and offered him the pad and pencil. He took them and she brushed her hand over his slowly, with pressure.

He flushed and looked down and away and over at his uncle, who was turning slowly red.

"Thank you again," she whispered to him.

"You're w-welcome," he said. "I really h-have to go..."

She stood aside, and let him rush to his uncle's side. The man looked like he was going to swat the boy, but gave her what she assumed was a dirty look. The huge, bubble-like glasses covered his eyes so well she couldn't see them.

She watched them shove through the crowd as her escort returned to her side with a glass of champagne.

"Well?" He whispered.

"Contact," she said.

3

An hour later, dinner was announced. The guests slowly made their way into a lavish banquet hall, where porters seated them according to a chart. She sampled the fish and made small talk with the other women at her table while the men ate, smoked cigars, and ubiquitously drank whiskey and water. Catherine realized quickly that these women were either vapid through breeding or purpose.

Any of them could be a plant, like she was, or all of them. For all she knew, no one at this formal occasion was what they seemed. The whole room seemed a microcosm of her professional life. She smiled and bantered mindlessly, all the while keeping the squat ambassador and his charmingly hapless nephew in sight.

She patiently endured the Ambassador's hand on her thigh, skin inwardly crawling at his touch, but outwardly giggling and simpering every time he let it be known to the table what he was doing. She dutifully swatted at his hand but made no effort to move it. She fit right in.

Then the MC called for everyone's attention. The

Ambassador excused himself and stood. His speech would be in a moment. Out of the corner of her eye, Catherine watched the grumpy diplomat noisily stand up and begin sauntering across the floor with a huge Cuban cigar in hand, already lit, headed for the balcony overlooking the circular drive and the woods lining Grosvenor Square.

She applauded politely when the Ambassador took the podium, where he began a speech about cooperation and the spirit of the West. Half of the people in the room rolled their eyes, and the others loved it, primarily because they *were* the West.

Catherine dabbed her mouth with a napkin and excused herself to the ladies'. Two of the five men at her table rose, proving that chivalry and manners were alive and well.

Moving sedately, she exited the hall. She watched the aide from the corner of her eye. He saw her rise and did the same.

She stopped at the bar and accepted another glass of champagne. The sandy-haired aide exited the hall and closed the door on the spirited applause from within. She smiled at him, set her drink down, and retreated up the grand stairway, slowly walking across the balcony so recently occupied by the royal contingent. She stopped once, watching him. He strode up the stairs, taking them two at a time.

The two barmen smiled at each other and pretended not to see. The guards watched with undisguised interest but said nothing.

Catherine ducked through a door and started down a dimly lit row of locked offices. At the end of the hall, she waited.

The young man appeared. She winked at him and rounded the corner.

Down the row of doors, she looked for one unlocked. Room 213. She took a handkerchief from her clutch, opened the door, and closed it behind her, leaving the cloth sticking out of the closed door.

In the dark, she moved to the windows and reclined against the glass. She didn't look up into the corner of the room where a tiny light shone, affixed to a camera. She knew she was on security, and that was part of the op. It had to look like a little harmless necking.

The door opened and he slipped through, plucking her handkerchief from the door frame. He crossed the room and handed it to her. She accepted.

"Why, thank you, sir."

"You're w-welcome,"

She looked out of the window into the lighted drive below. A million pounds' worth of cars, lined neatly up. Guard patrols with guns and dogs moved through the trees. Footlights lit the Grosvenor Gardens beyond the lined drive. No one strolled there. They had cordoned the whole square for the gala, and the three streets around the embassy.

She looked back at him and reached out to toy with his tie.

"Nice night," she said softly.

"I-it is," he said. His slightly accented English was soft and uncertain.

She tugged on his tie. He leaned close to her. She pressed her lips against his cheek. His hands were on the wall and window as he leaned over her.

"You have something for me?" she said almost subvocally.

He didn't reply, but his hand went from the window to her shoulder. He pulled her into a rough embrace, and she allowed him to kiss her. They moved passionately, but with closed lips. His hand went to her dress and she felt, under his palm, a small hard object. He cupped her left breast, and she moved into the recess of his arms. While kissing her, his hand slipped the item into the small pocket of her exposed cleavage.

She put her hand over his and drew him in.

"T-three days," he whispered. "Coordinates of the troops, equipment manifests, e-everything I could f-find," His voice shook. She wrapped her arms around him and nuzzled his neck.

"Any message for our friend?" she asked.

He bent to nibble her ear. She reflected that his delicate skin was infinitely preferable to the Ambassador's florid complexion.

"*G-get me o-out!*" he hissed. "I-I can't do this anym-more. Get m-me out!"

She nodded slightly.

"I'll tell him. Now do it."

He whispered, "Thank y-you," and dropped his other hand to her arm and pressed her against the glass. She struggled, shaking her head as he tried to kiss her again.

"Mmmph. Mmmph!" She struggled and made a show of trying to get free of him. He was surprisingly strong. He tried to force her lips open, to slide his tongue into her mouth. She turned her head again, bucking.

"No! No!" She wiggled an arm free. "I said *no!*" She brought her left hand up swiftly and caught his cheek in an open-handed slap that resounded through the room, though it couldn't have hurt much.

He backed up, one hand pressed to his cheek. He winked at her, and she tried not to laugh.

"I-I thought you w-wanted to!"

"I… I don't know. I said *maybe! Maybe.* Not definitely. I thought you were nice. You aren't nice. I thought you were nice, but you aren't. Not at all! I want to go. Let me go!" She put her hands on her hips and made her voice shrill, but shaky, as though she were scared of him. She didn't try to leave.

"Fine," he said. He turned to go. "Who wants y-you anyhow?" He stalked through the darkened room to the door. "W-who needs the a-aggravation?"

She sniffed, a tear forming. Crying on cue was just one of her myriad skills. She sobbed once and choked as though holding back a flood.

"Wait!" she cried and tried to run after him. She stumbled over a chair and almost fell.

He paused at the door and looked at her. "F-forget it. I'm g-going."

She reached the door. The camera would show nothing out of the ordinary, a tryst gone wrong. When she vanished, he would raise the alarm. They'd try to use the video to reconstruct who she was, but it would all lead back to a dead end. Even when they did trace her back to the Ambassador, they would find that the abandoned apartment in which she supposedly lived. The gloves she had worn since before getting into the Ambassador's limousine ensured no fingerprints. The prints they would find in the apartment weren't hers.

The Ambassador would have deniability, and the diplomat with whose secrets she was absconding would not blame his nephew. Or at least, would blame him but not suspect him. She let him get a head start, pretending to wipe away tears for the camera.

All that remained was strolling out the front door, and making her meet at the boat, where she would deliver the key to the Commander, and be on the next plane to New York.

Part of the deal was the stipulation that her people get first look at the information before passing it on to the Ambassador. Gratitude had a short half-life in the intelligence community, and the golden rule was 'cover thy ass'.

She yanked the door open, following after him. He was halfway back to the main hall. She followed slowly, keeping up the appearance for the cameras. She rounded the corner and was back on the balcony.

She saw he was far ahead of her, in fact, all the way into the foyer, with the Marine guards. The Marine guards, and the squat Diplomat with the huge cigar and horrible manners.

Why-

For a moment, she thought she could see fear and sadness in his eyes, but his voice carried to her, and she knew in an instant what had happened. She didn't even have time to swear.

"T-that's her!" His voice was strong, and more heavily accented now. "That's the woman! She's g-g-got my key, uncle! She took it from m-m-me while we… we were a-alone!"

The fat diplomat's heavily accented shout was punctuated with the pointed cigar. "Guards! Seize the woman! She is a thief! Spy! Seize her!"

The Marine guards looked at their commander, who nodded. The guards began jogging up the stairs to the balcony. Catherine didn't hesitate. She ran.

4

She rounded the corner, and flew down the hall, running on the balls of her feet. She heard the guards behind her and slid around a corner. She stopped for two valuable seconds and snapped the heels off her expensive shoes. Better.

She ran.

She didn't blame the shy, sweet aide. He looked terrified. Obviously, his Uncle had caught him coming down, and he had made up the story to cover his ass. It didn't bode well for her, but that was *her* lookout. He was only worried about himself. Given the shockingly short life expectancy of the family members that had held the position before him, each pressed into service one after the other, he had good reason. Whatever deal he had worked out with the Ambassador, she hoped he lived to reap the benefits.

She came to a stairwell. She kicked open the door then ducked across the hall. She slipped into the men's restroom and closed the door quietly behind her. She heard the guards round the corner as the stairwell door slammed shut. They kicked it open and split up; one ran up the stairs to the next floor, the other down. She left the restroom and ran back the way she came, skidding to a halt at the corner of the hall and checking before running across. She stopped at the end of the hall. A window looked over the back of the building. Fifteen feet below the window was the tarred low roof of the back of the embassy. She considered the drop.

The stairway door slammed open behind her. She was out of time. Backing up, she threw herself at the window, curling into a ball. Capable of stopping high-velocity sniper rounds, the panes of glass were glazed and bulletproof. The embassy was old, however, and scheduled to be demolished as soon as the new building was completed. She hit the window and punched the entire pane out, tumbling after it.

She tucked into the roll as best as she could, but she hit hard on her right side. She gasped in pain as a rib let go, but went with her momentum. The pane of glass slammed down beside her, still in one piece. She looked up in time to see the guards raising their rifles. She crawled under the glass as the bullets slammed into the tar around her. The thick glass stopped four shots, starring the glass and pounding the displaced speed of the rounds into her body.

She crawled to the edge of the roof and looked over. It was ten feet to the ground. She rolled off the roof into a four-point crouch.

She had seconds before the guards and dogs were after her. She darted for the shadows at the edge of the poorly-lit loading area.

She thought furiously as she ran. Her retrieval point was the dock at Serpentine River, two miles west of the Embassy, down Park Lane, across Hyde Park. If she could make it to the trees, she had a chance.

The broken rib jabbed her side with each breath and footstep. She heard yells and barking close behind. She vaulted over the concrete barricade and pelted down Culcross street. She stayed in the lee of the buildings, trying to hold to shadows. There were no people on the street, both a blessing and curse. No one would point and say "She ran that way!" However, no citizens in the field of fire meant the Marines might shoot.

She had a long run ahead of her and concentrated on speed. She skidded to a halt at the end of Culcross. She risked a glance behind her. There were figures running after her. Marines and some other team of guards, likely the diplomat's bodyguards.

She ran left down the one-way Park Lane. She was running with traffic and passing a few late-night pedestrians. She cut a curious figure, a woman in a red dress running hell-bent down the road in expensive, now-ruined dress shoes. She laughed. Absurd.

She crossed Park Lane, Stopped on the meridian. She waited for a break in the oncoming traffic and crossed the second lane. She was almost to Lover's Fountain. If she could lose herself in the trees, she was fine. The pain in her side was considerable, but she had suffered far worse.

She headed for the trees on the far side of the fountain when a vehicle skidded to a halt alongside her and three Marines leaped out. They pulled weapons up into firing stances, and she altered her path. She barreled right into them, knocking one down and side-kicking another in the belly. His air whooshed out, and he dropped his rifle.

The third raised his sidearm. Catherine didn't hesitate. She knocked the weapon aside and drove her elbow into the hollow of his throat. He made a choking sound as she grabbed the gun with both hands and twirled away, wrenching it from his hand.

Only seconds had passed. She wobbled, recovered her footing, and ran on. Her Krav Maga instructors would be proud. She had altered killing moves to suit the moment. She had disabled three armed men and disarmed two of them. Zero body count. These weren't bad men; they were soldiers doing a job. It wasn't their fault they didn't know whose side she was on.

She bolted across the tree line.

She had officially crossed the line. The crack of the rifle told her she was off the detail list and had moved to the 'shoot to kill' list. A bullet slammed into a tree near her. She didn't know how close and didn't care to find out.

She ran right, crossing out of the tree line into the boardwalk of Hyde Park. She ran past small booths and people strolling among the amusements. She was getting looks now. She dodged between the concession and the trees, heading for the water.

There were vehicles behind her, and men on foot. She had a squad after her, maybe two. There would be London Metro after her, too. She wondered briefly how the Ambassador would explain an international incident away. It wasn't her problem, she decided.

Dirt hissed up at her feet. She was clear of the boardwalk and was on open ground again. The trees were thinner here, and she cut in and out, hoping the scant cover would suffice.

She smelled water.

Another shout and more bullets. She ducked into the reeds and bushes near the water's edge. She heard the *wheet!* of bullets as she dodged through the underbrush and leaped through the last of the branches into the cold, waiting water of the Serpentine River. She felt the wig pull off as she hit the water. She swam with powerful strokes until her lungs burned, staying under as long as she could.

Slowly she drifted to the surface and broke only enough to draw air into her lungs through her nose. She watched the shore carefully, seeing frenzied movement, but no pursuit. Unless they dived in after her, she was safe. She turned over and swam, trying to cause as small a wake as possible. Fifty meters from shore, she saw the dim light of a small craft's stern. She made for it and was soon reaching over the side of the rail, gasping in pain as she banged her side against the boat.

Hands pulled her over the side of the small craft into the boat as the driver dropped the lever. He pushed the big diesel engines to full, beginning a race along the Serpentine. They headed for the Long River, and their waiting escort to the jet.

She dropped her commandeered pistol on the deck and reached into the bodice of her dress. She pulled the USB key out and handed it to Captain Amit, who immediately took it forward to slot it into a waiting laptop for encrypted transmission.

She looked up at Commander Halevy, her handler. He was also an old family friend, which neither of them let on while in uniform or, in her case, working clothes.

She dragged herself to her feet, water seeping from the bedraggled and ruined gown. The expensive fabric was torn under the arms and up each thigh from her run and covered with river water and mud. Her hair stuck to her face and there were scratches down both arms from where she had leaped through the trees into the river. She pressed her rib with one hand, wincing, and she saluted him with the other.

"Mission accomplished, sir."

He smiled warmly at her. "Excellent work, Major." He looked her up and down. "Enjoy your evening?"

"Some plum," Catherine said, with a wry smile.

The End

To find out more about Aaron S Gallagher
and his books, visit
www.indiesunited.net/aaron-gallagher

Timed Out

by Guy Thair

Eric

Eric Kraus stared at the blinking yellow, "NOT READY" light on his internet modem for the fiftieth time in five minutes and swore under his breath.

Where the bloody hell was that sodding repairman? He'd called them nearly three hours ago, they were bloody useless.

He abruptly stood up and stamped into the kitchen of his tiny seventh floor apartment, banging cupboards and slamming drawers, taking out his frustration on inanimate objects while he waited for the kettle to boil.

Eric poured himself a cup from the brew of cheap, bitter coffee he'd been reduced to drinking lately, sipping it whilst gazing blankly into the mostly empty fridge, before closing the door and trudging back into the living room/bedroom/office, sitting down in front of his monitor and jiggling the mouse in that universal, impatient manner of computer users everywhere.

The screen saver materialised and he clicked on the cloud storage icon marked "Novel", opening the manuscript he'd spent the previous six weeks editing, only now happy that the final draft could be sent to his publisher.

And stared.

Then he stared some more, just to be sure.

The page was blank.

At the top, an innocuous little red banner said:

"Auto-refresh failed. Server session timed out, please check your internet connection and try again."

"No! No no no no no no!"

No, this couldn't be, he couldn't have lost it.

Two years of work! Six hellish weeks of rewrites and editing!

He frantically clicked the refresh button, willing his words to reappear on the empty expanse of white, but to no avail.

Eric felt the rage building up inside him.

He stood up, his chair toppling backwards onto the cluttered coffee table behind him, sending the accumulated pile of unwashed plates, take-out containers, and beer cans in all directions, though he barely registered the sound of smashing crockery, so consumed was he with incandescent fury that his masterpiece had been wiped from existence in one split second by that…that, thing!

His enraged glare fell on the implacable, blinking yellow light, still silently proclaiming that the modem was NOT READY to connect him to the internet, then on his out of date, obsolete computer tower, not even capable of doing something as simple as saving his manuscript reliably, hence his initially hesitant decision to upload it to "The Cloud", whatever the hell that was.

Eric looked down at his desk for a moment, then calmly picked up the unfinished cup of horrible coffee and, very deliberately, poured it into the back of his monitor, taking great satisfaction in the loud bang and acrid smoke that followed.

He ripped the cables from the tower unit, picked it up, marched across the room and unceremoniously dumped the whole thing out the window.

He didn't even stop to watch but was rewarded a few seconds later by the resounding crash as it smashed on the vacant lot next to his apartment block.

Eric stood in the middle of his trashed room for a minute or two, quietly sniveling, then he pulled himself together, shrugged into his leather jacket, grabbed his wallet, and went out to get drunk, slamming the door behind him.

Remembering there was construction work in progress on the ground floor, he ignored the elevators and took the stairs, leaving through the rear door and making for the nearest bar.

Several hours and more than a few drinks later, Eric weaved his way back from whichever dive he'd finished his crawl in, returning via the front entrance now the workmen had left for the night.

He was standing, gently swaying, as he waited for the elevator, he heard footsteps crossing the half-completed lobby.

When he turned, he saw two serious-looking policemen, one of whom held out his identification and said;

"Mr. Kraus, Eric Kraus?" Eric nodded, a puzzled frown beginning to form on his already befuddled face, "Eric Kraus, I am arresting you for the murder of Michael Fleming, you do not have to say anything, but anything you do say...."

"What? What?!" Eric couldn't deal with this, not today, of all days, "What the bloody hell are you on about? And who the hell is Michael Fleming?"

Michael

The afternoon traffic was terrible, the heat was horrible, the pollen count was making his head feel like it was stuffed with glue and cotton wool, and then, to top it all off, he had to go and deal with ignorant shitheads like this – he glanced at the job sheet on the seat next to him – Eric fucking Kraus, some idiot customer who had already rung three times, each time ruder than the last, whining about his bloody modem not connecting. He was betting it was because the cheap bastard used some budget price provider with a crappy signal and there was nothing wrong with his computer at all.

Some people, thought Michael Fleming, I.T. genius and all-round computer whizz-kid, some people need turning off and then not turning back on again.

He chuckled at his own joke as he inched forward another few yards and after ten minutes he finally pulled over outside the address on his clipboard and climbed out, retrieving his case and locking the van.

He walked up to the entrance, but there appeared to be work going on, a large hoarding with apologies from the building firm for any inconvenience and advice to use the rear entrance during work hours.

Michael took a step back, looked up at the front of the tall block, and consulted his clipboard again, noticing for the first time that the shithead Kraus lived on the seventh floor.

"Oh great, that means bloody stairs I suppose," he saw that there was an empty lot to the left of the building and started walking around that way, looking for the rear door, "why can't all the fucking idiots live on the first floor..."

Michael Fleming had still been grumbling about moronic customers when he was struck by a computer tower, travelling at what forensic experts later calculated to be approximately eighty miles per hour.

That evening, in a badly disheveled room on the seventh floor, a small yellow light went out and was replaced by a green one that said "READY".

To find out more about Guy Thair and his books, visit
www.indiesunited.net/guy-thair

Walkabout

A Cadillac Holland Short

by H. Max Hiller

I have a seventy-pound pit bull named Roux as an unofficial partner. He was the primary murder suspect in the first homicide I investigated. I was able to establish that he was only the murder weapon, but I was still supposed to have had him euthanized. I chose instead to change his name and have a trainer work the homicidal triggers out of him. I figured that if a Tier One military operative like myself could learn not to kill people as a first response to aggression, then a dog could do so as well. I was fighting an uphill battle to have Roux designated as a K-9 officer with my captain at the State Police. Captain Hammond's resistance was based as much on not liking me personally as it was on not wanting to have a valuable State Police K-9 team assigned to NOPD.

Roux and I walk the French Quarter twice a day, once in the morning and once again late in the afternoon. I never wear a uniform, and I keep my badge and Glock under a loose shirt or jacket so I blend in rather than stick out. These walks are when I get to speak with the locals who make up my network of informants in the Quarter. Most of them are street vendors and musicians, starving artists, members of street performance groups, or part of the city's homeless population. These characters are the eyes and ears nobody pays much attention to, but they are also the ones who might overhear or see anything that is out of order in the roughly eighty square blocks we all call home. I also know, and am recognized by, bartenders, servers, strippers, and street hustlers, either from my partnership in the bistro and from my willingness to take their side in most beefs with drunken or otherwise unruly customers. I keep much of what they say to myself for later use, but any actionable tips they provide get passed along to Chief Avery.

I also know just about every dope dealer, pickpocket, short change artist, and petty thief working the Quarter. I leave them alone to do their business because arresting them creates a vacuum some stranger would fill. It is handy to know whose tree to shake if a bad batch of heroin hits the street, the wrong wallet gets poached, or something of a little too much value suddenly goes missing. I learned the value of informant networks when I worked in intelligence, which seems like an entirely different lifetime ago. The experience of having access to cutting-edge technology taught me that the best photograph of two people talking could never tell me the topic of their discussion. That was something only a server or bartender might overhear, just as a petty thief might spot something through a car window that a drone would miss because it could only see from directly above.

The route that Roux and I follow varies slightly because that career also taught me the importance of not being predictable to my potential enemies. I like to walk Roux just after sunrise, but I gave him another outing so I could show Hardy's picture to my favorite contacts.

"We good to go?" I asked Roux as he did his usual hind leg dance after he peed on the bare ground of the neutral ground on Esplanade.

Roux trotted ahead of me, staying barely three feet ahead so he didn't strain against the four feet of slack in his heavy leather leash. We walked towards the river, past the Old Mint building, and then turned to the right to walk through the

French Market. Dogs are not particularly welcome in the crowded confines of the open-air flea market, but the vendors were all happy to see us and to give Roux a little scratch behind an ear or to rub his squared off head. We discussed how business was, the mood of the tourists on this particular weekend, and any problems they were having with shoplifters or were involved in any turf wars with the other vendors.

"Anyone getting counterfeit bills that you know of?" I asked Glenda, one of the dozens of merchants selling their wares under the market's long metal awning. She moved here from Arkansas after choosing this as her new home because her custom-made jewelry and necklaces sell better here than they ever did in Eureka Springs.

"Nobody has said anything. Is there something I should know?" she asked in return. I pulled Hardy's photo from my pocket and showed it to her. She did not recognize him, as did not one of the other vendors I would show it to, by the time Roux and I walked through the blocks-long French Market. All this meant was that Hardy did not plan to take any trinkets back to Hollywood after unloading his fake money. The price of most of this merchandise would also not have warranted using a fifty-dollar bill to make the sale, and his doing so would have drawn even more scrutiny of the bills than Jason and Juaquin gave what he tried to pass at Strada Ammazarre.

Roux and I crossed North Peters Street as we approached the gilded statue of Joan of Arc, to pass through a doorway in the floodwall. Roux likes to sniff his way along the train tracks beside the riverbank. I like that this path avoids the heavy tourist foot traffic along this stretch of tightly packed shops and cafes lining North Peters and Decatur Street. It also gives me an excuse to speak with the French Quarter's largest gathering of homeless people. There is a permanent population of veterans, and occasional runaway teenagers, who occupy the Moonwalk and Jackson Square after dark, but who move down by the river during the daytime to make way for the tourists and locals because the city doesn't want them within sight of the "good people" there to spend money.

I owe my life to a couple of the Vietnam-era vets that have been living here since my father was still on the force. They had tipped me off to a surveillance team being run by some people I was actively trying to force out of town. I don't know that there was intent to harm me or my family, but I do know that the way Tony and I dismantled the team disrupted whatever *was* being planned. Darnell and Boomer would have been retired and nearly through with paying off their mortgages if they had chosen to get a steady job and put a roof over their heads instead of using the city's slim pickings of shelters and food banks to survive. They both have beards that show their age, ponytail length hair, and wardrobes that would benefit much more from being replaced than laundered. Neither of them will discuss having served as Marines in Vietnam during the late Sixties and early Seventies, and neither of them ever asks about my own service in Special Operations and the classified intelligence work I did in Afghanistan and Iraq. We simply recognize and respect one another's personal hells.

"Does this guy look at all familiar?" I asked the pair and the handful of others they were standing with. One of the teenaged girls, I figured her to be about fifteen, busied herself with petting Roux. She tried to keep me from getting a good look at her face.

"He's been around a couple of nights. He had a different woman with him each time. I saw him over by Muriel's once and a couple of times at Café du Monde, late," Boomer spoke up. He handed the picture back to me as he spoke. Boomer was an artilleryman at Khe Sanh, which I learned from an NOPD patrolman who had run his name through the VA database after detaining him on a vagrancy charge that was immediately dropped. He lives in the open because two separate hooches he had at Khe Sanh received direct hits from Viet Cong artillery, killing most of his friends. His nerves simply don't last long indoors. He is tall and lean in a not very athletic way, and firing that many artillery rounds left him with hearing so bad that he shouts to hear himself talk. I have learned to take a step back rather than let him see me flinch whenever he speaks.

"Different women?" I repeated. Darnell caught what I was asking.

"I've seen one of them carrying a gym bag into Rick's before," he elaborated. Rick's Cabaret is one of the better established, and practically reputable, gentlemen's clubs on Bourbon Street. Most strippers carry their outfits in gym bags and look like they might be on their way to exercise or to cheerleader practice instead of to places like Rick's.

Rick's would not be a wise place to throw around counterfeit money. I now had a second thing to look into that might lead me to whoever worked over Hardy. I did not believe that the beating from a bouncer or enforcer of any given gentleman's club would have taken on the grievous and time-consuming nature of what happened in that hotel room. Dead men can't benefit from the lesson of a sound thrashing.

"Thanks, fellas," I said and acted as though I was starting to walk away. I nodded my head towards Darnell and he stepped in beside me as we put our backs to the others, especially the young girl who had been petting Roux. "I see you have a new friend."

"She's from Denver. She says her folks took to fighting all the time. Mom up and left and daddy began looking around the house for someone to take Mom's place. She chose not to play that game," he filled me in. "You going to send someone around for her?"

"Are you guys good with watching her back for now?" I wasn't going to do nothing, but doing what was expected of me would not help her at all.

"Yeah, we'll keep her close. She says her name is Annie," he informed me. I pulled about sixty bucks in folded bills from my pocket and handed him half of it without counting. He would not accept all of it, at least not all at once, but he was willing to take 'a little' to keep her fed and out of trouble. Taking all of it looked and felt too much like charity he didn't want.

There was no point in showing Hardy's photo to the servers at Café du Monde because they were not the ones who might have seen him. I would need to stop back by in the pre-dawn hours to see who might remember him. Sadly, the cafe was the perfect place to have passed his phony money. The servers make their own change, and most of them probably have no idea how to spot a really good fake bill. It takes a special kind of a jerk to rip somebody off for coffee and donuts and to take their good money in change.

I tugged on the leash and let Roux get his lead on me as we walked up the stairs and onto the Moonwalk's observation platform. Jackson Square lay directly across Decatur Street. The former Jax Brewery, now a stack of luxury condominiums, was to my left and Café du Monde to the right. There was a sizeable crowd on the steps below us watching a troupe of very limber Black youths do a set of break dancing and gymnastics in anticipation of collecting some decent tips for the effort. There was a sad chance that I might be chasing one of these boys down later that night after he tried to make up for whatever money these honest efforts did not earn by robbing some drunken tourist who staggered away from Bourbon Street. I doubted that many in the audience realized this was a skilled profession and not just a hobby for these kids. The odds of Hardy dropping a generous looking tip in their hat was slim, so I just gave a nod to the one who was running the boom box and keeping up the non-stop circus barker patter. He smiled at me and nodded back. It looked like they were having a good day.

The weather was clear and warm and Jackson Square was packed. There was another group of acrobats on the Cathedral side of the square, and people were standing two and three deep looking at the paintings and what-not the vendors hung from the heavy cast iron fence that surrounded the square's lush garden. I walked Roux across the square rather than try to negotiate a way through the throngs alongside the Pontalba Buildings. Actually, most people get nervous seeing a big pit bull on a leash and instinctively open a path for us. I did not admonish Roux for taking a moment to lift a leg and claim the statue of Andrew Jackson for his own. There are plenty of people in New Orleans who want to do far worse to the statue, unwilling to balance his having saved the city from British invasion against his egregiously genocidal campaigns against Native Americans and his being a slave owner. I know to hold my tongue in their company because I don't have a record that holds up well against such narrow judgment either.

We emerged onto the slate paving stones in front of St. Louis Cathedral and paused for a moment to rest Roux's feet. We had walked almost a mile on hard surfaces that had to be a little warm to his touch in this April sunshine. I took a seat on one of the metal park benches and he jumped up to sit next to me. I have no idea where he learned to sit in a chair like a human, but it is rather adorable. I pulled a bottle of water out of the messenger bag I carry anywhere I go and gave him as much of it as he wanted. I think he wound up slobbering as much as he gulped down.

Our unscheduled patrol led us down the Pirate's Alley side of the Cathedral to Royal Street. I glanced into a stand-up bar next to the Faulkner Museum. The bar is my late-night emergency rendezvous spot with Chief Avery, but I don't know any of the daytime staff. It is hard to make something a hiding place if everyone knows you go there. The only time Avery and I ever meet at the bar is when we don't want to be noticed. I have similar spots arranged with my sister, Katie, Tony, and a handful of informants who need to be certain nobody knows they speak with me. I meet them after we exchange a text message consisting of a single word that identifies the sender. The word also lets us both know the time and the place to meet. This small thing is among the handful of pieces of tradecraft from my past life that has translated well to my chosen line of work as a detective. It also weirds the heck out of everyone that has an arrangement like this with me. They all say it makes them feel like spies, which they are in a way.

Royal Street is famous for its open-air galleries, antique shops selling merchandise half the age of the building the store was in, and street musicians talented enough to be headliners in concert halls anywhere else on the planet. The mixture creates a particular sort of cacophony over and above what the rest of the Quarter generates on any given afternoon. Part of the street gets barricaded off from vehicular traffic during the day, and there were street musicians and artists vying for attention and dollars every block for three blocks in any direction from the micro-grocery on the corner of Royal and St. Peter that locals still call The A&P. The national grocery chain used to operate the store, but it was now being run as an outlet of a local company called Rouse's. The store is among the last handful of grocery stores that have survived the French Quarter's transformation from being an affordable working-class residential neighborhood to being not much more than a collection of pied-a-terre and vacation rentals. There are still people who live in the French Quarter full time, but the rents and home prices attract a population that can afford to shop at Whole Foods and other markets outside of the Quarter. Most of these small stores rely upon selling knick-knacks like hot sauces and easily-shipped packages of local specialty items to tourists to survive. Central Grocery on Decatur Street has survived largely on its reputation for muffaletta sandwiches, as opposed to trading on its shady past as a front for a local Mob family. My father used to complain about how much he missed the Quarter's old days.

I tossed five bucks into the guitar case of a musician strumming Mister Bojangles for the ten-thousandth time. Bobby was scruffy enough that he could make the song sound autobiographical. I palmed the photo to show it to him as I leaned over to drop the bill in his guitar case. He gave it an honest look before he shook his head and then he looked at the folded bill and grinned. Big bills attract other big bills in tip jars. It's why most performers toss a few tens and twenties of their own into the kitty when they start the day. I lead Roux around the corner onto Orleans Avenue and continued making our way towards Bourbon Street. I waved at the woman behind the counter of the coffee bean shop mid-way down the block. It is where I buy my own coffee, but it was not a place I figure would have been one of Hardy's victims during his spending spree.

I was developing a sense for how the guy likely spent the bulk of his bogus fifties. Hardy seems to have spent lavishly upon memories, be it strippers or good food and wine, rather than physical things. I was going to ask Detective Bassett whether there were any tourist trinkets found in the hotel room. I did not remember seeing even a single strand of cheap plastic beads in the brief time I was at the crime scene. It was as if Hardy both did not want to be reminded of where he had been and favored places where he was not likely to be remembered. It meant there was a pattern and motive to his actions, and it was going to be interesting to figure it out.

Bourbon Street in the daylight is nothing at all like it is when a dazzling rainbow of neon illuminates the bars and clubs lining its first nine blocks at midnight. The daytime profusion of families with strollers and young children makes it a profoundly different place. There is also something not quite right, maybe even unacceptable, about anyone walking down the street with a quart of beer in a massive plastic cup emblazoned with Big Ass Beer down its side at two in the afternoon anytime except during college football season. It is one of those things that makes perfect sense when the street is full of night-time revelers and someone thinks they can save money by buying a quart of cheap beer at a walk-up bar without considering what it will cost to get into a place with a bathroom an hour later. Probably half the arrests NOPD makes in the Quarter every night are for some fashion of public urination by people too drunk or stupid to think things through. Then again, who comes to Bourbon Street to think at all?

Bourbon Street would have been another perfect place for Hardy to have passed his fake fifty-dollar bills. An economy based almost entirely upon separating fools and their money was not very likely to question anybody spending money like a fool. I could not begin to imagine the number of times Hardy might have slapped down counterfeit money and either been intentionally shortchanged by a titty-dancer or overcharged by a bartender in a dimly lit nightclub. The joke was on everyone at the moment, but not everyone was still laughing when the money was counted come sunrise.

I opted to cut the walk short. Normally we would have worked our way across the Quarter as far as Rampart Street. The street was the northern border of the original city, and it was just two blocks beyond Bourbon Street. An interesting point of fact is that the French Quarter may well be the only place in all of New Orleans where a compass works right. Esplanade Avenue is geographically the eastern border of the

Quarter, but it runs north and south. Elysian Fields, which begins where these two streets intersect at a right angle just past the French Market, also runs north and south. Iberville is the quarter's modern-day western border, though most tourists still believe the line is drawn at Canal Street. Canal Street is its own oddity, having been named for a commercial canal that has never been built. There is a neighborhood at the far end of St. Charles Avenue called Riverbend. Carrollton Avenue is the backbone of this district, and it runs north from the river, the same as Esplanade. These two avenues never waver in their paths, but the pair still manage to intersect in the middle of town, at Bayou St. John, because of the city's crescent shape. And don't ask me to explain why a part of town called the Westbank sits on the east side of the Mississippi River. You learn to accept such things or you go crazy, and when you learn to accept things this simple you also learn to accept a lot of things about living here that will never be fixed or properly explained.

Roux and I walked down Bourbon Street towards Governor Nicholls, where we would turn right and head home. We passed Lafitte's Blacksmith Shop, the city's oldest bar, and also walked by the home of Dr. Norman McSwain. He is the city's official police surgeon, so he is called upon anytime an officer is shot or wounded in the line of duty. Doctor McSwain helped create the in-field trauma protocols and training that saved my life in Iraq when Tony and I were ambushed. His address is stored in my mental map of the Quarter in case I need faster medical care than calling an ambulance might provide. The Quarter is home to other surgeons at Tulane's medical school that I know I can call upon as well. Katie is probably right to view my knowing where to get medical help of this caliber on the fly as another manifestation of my PTSD, but she also concedes that she may be grateful if I ever need to act upon the knowledge.

I trailed behind Roux as we walked the last few blocks towards home, with my mind far more on Crenshaw Hardy than on Roux continuing to mark every vertical surface he could find. Roux wanted to make it absolutely clear to every other four-legged animal in the Quarter that they were trespassing on his turf. It was no different than my having just alerted the neighborhood's two legged creatures that I was on the hunt in the tight confines of our shared neighborhood.

Community policing, and even the very idea of foot patrols, has fallen out of favor since my father joined the New Orleans Police Department in the 1960s. Hopefully, someday the powers that be will realize that all the expensive high-tech gadgetry and computer algorithms will never give them the lay of the land the way that a uniformed foot patrol's connections with the people in a neighborhood does. The average NOPD officer who spends some time shooting the breeze in a Seventh Ward barbershop on a Saturday morning will have spent their time better than had they spent that same time behind the wheel of a patrol car cruising the neighborhood with the windows rolled up.

Sigh. Thinking this way is why Chief Avery has relegated me to work alone. Keeping me, and my thoughts on such things, at a distance is his way of keeping me from antagonizing the department that pays his salary.

To find out more about H. Max Hiller
and his books, visit
www.indiesunited.net/h-max-hiller

Thank you for taking the time to read this collection from the authors of Indies United Publishing House. We hope you enjoyed it and would like to encourage you to take a moment to review this collection on your favorite reading platform.

A little about Indies United

Here at Indies United, we are a co-op of like-minded authors working together to showcase our books and highlight our diversity as writers. We openly encourage and support both new and established authors in their pursuit of finding their audience while bringing to you books worth reading. Our goal is to give authors a home to call their own, while bringing fresh, innovative, and exciting books to readers all over the world.

If you are an author, please check us out at www.indiesunited.net

If you would like to connect to Indies United you can find us at:

Facebook
https://www.facebook.com/IndiesUnitedPublishing
OR @IndiesUnitedPublishing

Twitter
https://twitter.com/IndiesUnitedPub
OR @IndiesUnitedPub

Instagram
https://www.instagram.com/lisaorbanauthor/

Linkedin
www.linkedin.com/in/indies-united-publishing-house

Pinterest
https://www.pinterest.com/indiesunited/

GoodReads
https://www.goodreads.com/user/show/122472367-indies-united

www.ingramcontent.com/pod-product-compliance
Lightning Source LLC
Chambersburg PA
CBHW070628310726
48982CB00001B/200
* 9 7 8 1 6 4 4 5 6 3 9 6 0 *